Winter's Tales

NEW SERIES: 2

Winter's Tales

NEW SERIES: 2

*

EDITED BY

Robin Baird-Smith

St. Martin's Press

New York

ISBN 0–312–00085–5
Library of Congress Catalog Card No. 86–042905

First U.S. Edition
10 9 8 7 6 5 4 3 2 1

CONTENTS

ACKNOWLEDGEMENTS

INTRODUCTION

This is the second in Constable's new series of *Winter's Tales*. The reception given to last year's volume on both sides of the Atlantic by the critics was very generous and has encouraged us to offer this new collection of short stories. We hope now to make this an annual event.

In this present volume, I have included stories by authors with established reputations as well as many by authors who have first had their work published in volume form in *Winter's Tales*. Each category of writer is as important to the collection as the other. But, as last year, I have extended the scope of *Winter's Tales* to include one or two writers whose first language is not English. This year there is a short story by Jorge Luis Borges and one which has been specially written for the book by Michel Tournier – a writer of genius, in my view, who does not enjoy the reputation in this country that he deserves.

Many reviewers of the last volume of *Winter's Tales* commented on the unusual variety of the stories in the book, their length, style and mood. Maybe this variety is even greater in the second volume. I hope that this may be seen to be one of the virtues of *Winter's Tales*, for we never insist on any specific length or theme.

Finally, I would like to express my thanks to Alan Maclean whose inspiration it was to publish the first volume of *Winter's Tales* under the Macmillan imprint in 1955 and who kindly suggested that Constable might revive the collection with this new series.

Robin Baird-Smith

Constable, 1986

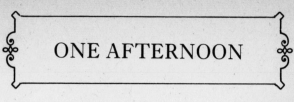

ONE AFTERNOON

Rachel Billington

It was so hot the leaves were stuck together like sweaty fingers. They touched the window where Daniel lay. He had pulled his bed close, lay sprawling, looking for air. Puff. He blew out his cheeks and then pressed them in again with his fingers. The flesh felt firm like an over-stuffed cushion.

He began to touch other parts of his body, noting the texture and shape as if it were not his own.

'What are you doing?' Rosemary stood at the doorway. Aggressive as ever. Nosey too.

'Reading.' Daniel picked up *Point Counter Point* and flapped it over his head.

'Why are you only wearing shorts?'

'Because it's hot.' Stupid, stupid girl. 'Anyway, they're not shorts, they're pants.' There wasn't much hope of shocking her. They'd been brought up as brother and sister for the last seven years.

'They're not very nice.' Rosemary came closer. She stood over him with a derisory smile. 'I only like white underwear.'

She was pretty, Daniel thought objectively. In a seventeen-year-old way. With clear skin and shiny hair and roundness everywhere. He'd seen her often enough in the bath to know, though she'd grown rather coy lately.

'I'm stifling!' He rolled over on his stomach. Her breasts were tipped by the palest pink.

Rosemary sat on the bed. 'Do you want to touch me?' She sounded serious.

Daniel put out his hand without looking and grasped

what he thought must be her thigh. 'Now I've touched you,' he said mockingly. Then he meant to let go and return to his book but the skin he felt was so smooth, like shiny wood, that he found his fingers gliding over it, backwards and forwards.

Was it really Rosemary's thigh? Under his fingers it seemed to become the convex of a spanish guitar, the model of a galleon, a desk top rolled without hinge.

He rolled over to have a look. There she sat, complacent as ever, wearing white shorts and a disgusting half-smile. That was new. She didn't often smile at him. And it was her thigh. He let go of it abruptly. Now he lay on his back, arms behind his head, staring at her.

'Why are you staring at me?' She shifted on the bed. Her thighs, spread flat by contact, elongated as they rose. Above her shorts she was wearing a white aertex shirt which meant she had been playing tennis.

'Did you win?'

'What?'

'Tennis. Did you win?'

'The sun was so bright.' She sank lower on the bed. So she hadn't won. 'Who were you playing anyway?'

'John.'

'That creep!'

'He's better than you at tennis.'

Daniel thought of the dialogue in *Point Counter Point*, the wit, the subtlety, inventiveness; never a repetition, never a dead-end. 'It's far too hot for playing tennis.'

'That's what I said.'

Why did he bother speaking to her at all? He had seen what she was like the very first day he'd come to this house. She'd been ten, he eleven. She was fair, neat, sturdy, the eldest of four children with the oldest girl's bossy self-possession. He was dark, thin, dumped on remote cousins by parents who thought he'd be better in healthy English country than with them abroad.

He looked at her under his arm. She was dragging off her tennis shoes, dropping them with a thump to the uncarpeted floor. He had been a threat to her: a year older and clever while she was stupid.

'Why are you so stupid?'

'If you're going to start up, I'm off.' She half-rose and again the thighs changed shape.

'No, don't go!' He grabbed at her and met the same sensation of polished wood. Living wood. It was better to bicker with her than lie in dissatisfied suffocation on his bed. The trouble with Huxley was that he went on and on. And *on*. He took his hand away as Rosemary settled down again. Now she was half-lying beside him.

She picked up the book, looked at it as if it were something from outer-space and then dropped it on the floor.

'You're an illiterate.' He put his hands back behind his head.

'You're a show-off. All those books and exams and scholarships. It's just showing-off.'

'You'd wipe away the whole of human endeavour towards understanding the universe?'

She gave a cackle. 'Honestly, Dan. You can't be that pompous.' There was a sweet smell about her, warm and grassy.

'By the time you're thirty you'll be a great lump of a woman with your brain all clogged up with nursery semolina and meetings in the village hall.'

'And what will you be?'

'Free.'

'Free!' She gave another cackle. 'You're so conceited. You're the most conceited person I know!' She crouched up now, bending over him so he could see how her breasts dropped downwards. He remembered what it felt like to hold a bunch of grapes cupped in his

[13]

hand.

'Touch me,' he said, grinning. 'It's your turn. I've touched you twice.' As he spoke he felt a tremendous throb under his pants which he was sure must be visible a mile away. A surge of heat washed over his neck and head. Rosemary must see now. But her expression was unchanged, a kind of careless concentration, he thought, pleased with the choice of words.

'Where shall I touch you?' Her voice was politely enquiring. Would she pinch him and run away as she had as a child?

'Wherever you like.' The scarlet heat seemed to have left him now for a pale inner trembling. He held up his hand in front of his eyes and it was quite steady. Yet he felt as if he was trembling all over.

'I'll put my hand over your heart. I love to feel hearts beating. I always wished my dolls had hearts.'

Daniel noticed her cheeks were a very deep pink, making her eyes bluer than ever, although they still wore the calculating look which so maddened him.

She laid her hand on his chest. 'Oooh!' she gasped. 'It's beating so hard I can hardly keep my hand on it. It'll bounce me right off if I'm not careful. How lovely! I do love hearts.' She fixed her blue eyes on Daniel. 'Can I put my head on it so I can listen as well as feel?' Daniel found he couldn't speak. His voice had gone underground, down in his body somewhere. He managed a grunt but Rosemary hadn't waited.

She lay forward across him, her breasts around waist level, her hair tickling his nostrils. 'It's wonderful!' she cried, her voice somewhat muffled.

Daniel brought his hands forward slowly and placed them under each breast. Rosemary didn't react, apart from little muffled cries of pleasure. She was so stupid. What did she think would happen if they went on like this? Or perhaps she wasn't so stupid.

Daniel felt her nipples harden through the aertex. They were like the little unripened grapes at the bottom of the bunch. He began to edge her shirt out of her shorts.

Rosemary sat up. Her eyes were vacant. 'I'm sweating,' she murmured, pulling up her shirt and pulling it right over her head. It wasn't the action of a stripper, rather of a gym mistress before her shower, but Daniel was past such distinctions.

In a moment, they were both naked and Rosemary's pinkness was covered by Daniel. So brief the moment.

So brief the moment. They lay on their backs side by side. Daniel prayed Rosemary would say nothing and she didn't. He realised he had closed his eyes or maybe he'd just lost vision but now they were open again, seeing so sharply, so clearly. The leaves by the window which had seemed fat-fingered, stubby, were now frilled with the filigree of lace. The colours, so drowsily dull, now glittered with silver-edged sunbeams. Yet, though he saw with precision, his body had the heaviness and tranquillity of still water. He closed his eyes slowly and then opened them again. He didn't want to sleep.

Rosemary moved a little at his side. Maybe he should say something. Thank you? He had never thanked her for anything in his life. 'Thank you.'

'What?'

Daniel cleared his throat. 'Thank you.' 'Oh.'

Oh. What did 'Oh' mean? Were things to be different between them or not?

They lay silent again. From outside the window came the sound of a car, crunching on the gravelled driveway.

'That might be Mummy.'

Perhaps her voice was a little gentler. Daniel could not bring himself to look at her and see her expression.

[15]

He didn't want her to be different. How could she be, after all? After all these years. Change would be false, disgusting.

And yet. Someone seemed to have taken the plug out of his tranquil water, leaving an echoing hole. What was he doing with this girl? 'You'd better get dressed.'

'So had you.' Her voice was sharp, almost bad-tempered.

Daniel's black hole felt a little less dangerous. In a moment he would be able to look at her. At least she was pretty. He remembered the weight of her breasts in his hands.

Rosemary sat up and began to get dressed. Daniel realised she was trying to avoid looking at him too.

'You'd better put something on.' Bossy tone.

'Yes.' He leant over and felt about for his pants.

Rosemary, quickly dressed, sat on the edge of the bed, running her fingers through her hair.

Daniel wondered if he should kiss her, show some sign of affection. They had not kissed once. On the other hand, he had thanked her and she had only said 'Oh'.

'Rosie! I'm back!' Her mother called from downstairs.

She stood up abruptly, her eyes suddenly scared.

'Take a bath.' Daniel gripped her hand. 'You played tennis.'

'Yes. Yes. I will.' She looked at him gratefully.

He smiled a little. Perhaps practical advice was better than a kiss. No hypocrisy. No love. He couldn't even think the word.

Rosemary stood at the door. She hesitated.

More was expected. There should be more. She was quite right. Daniel bent down as if to pick up his book but really he was hiding a ludicrous watering in his eyes. Well, it was natural to be emotional under the circumstances. First time. But not in front of her.

Still bent low, he mumbled in her direction, if indeed she was still there, he couldn't see her anymore, 'It was so hot.'

'Yes.' So she was there. 'That's why I'm going to have a bath.' The door closed carefully.

Daniel's fingers curled round the book and he climbed back onto the bed. Rethinking, he got off again, pulled back all the covers except the sheet and got in under it.

The sun had moved round so that now it filled the room with broad, flat strokes of gold. Although they passed over Daniel's head, he could feel them beating the air around him.

He pulled the sheet up over his face and entered a world of pure whiteness.

The book tipped off the edge of the bed.

SHAKESPEARE'S MEMORY

Jorge Luis Borges

Translated by Norman Thomas di Giovanni

There are ardent followers of Goethe or the Eddas or the plodding *Nibelungenlied*; Shakespeare has been my destiny. He still is, though in a way that nobody could have foretold except one person, Daniel Thorpe, who has just died in Pretoria. There is another man, but I have never seen his face.

I am Hermann Soergel. The inquisitive reader has perhaps browsed in my *Shakespeare Chronology*, which I once believed essential for a proper understanding of the text and which has been translated into several languages, including English. It is not impossible, therefore, that he may recall an ongoing polemic concerning a certain emendation that Theobald interpolated into his critical edition of 1734 and that from that date on has become an undisputed part of the canon. Today the uncivil tone of those almost antagonistic pages surprises me. Around 1914 I wrote – but never published – a study of the compound words which were wrought by the playwright and Greek scholar George Chapman for his translations of Homer and which takes English back, without his having suspected it, to its origin (*Ursprung*) – Anglo-Saxon. I never thought that Chapman's voice, which I have now forgotten, would be familiar to me. One or two offprints, I believe, signed with my initials, complete my literary biography. I do not know whether it is legitimate to include an unpublished translation of *Macbeth*, which I embarked upon to take my mind off the death of my brother Otto Julius, who fell on the western front in 1917. I never finished it; I saw that English, to its great benefit, has two registers at its disposal – the Germanic and the Latin – while our German, in spite of its greater music, is limited to but one.

I have already mentioned Daniel Thorpe. Major Barclay introduced me at a certain Shakespeare congress. I will mention neither the place nor the date, as I know very well that such incidentals are really beside the point.

What is more important is the fact that Daniel Thorpe's face, which my partial blindness has helped me to forget, was his glaring unhappiness. After years and years, a man can fake many things but not happiness. In an almost physical way, Daniel Thorpe exuded melancholy.

One night after a long session at the congress, we found ourselves in a pub. To give ourselves a true sense of being in England (where we were at the time), we drained ritual pewter tankards of warm, dark beer.

'In the Punjab,' said the major, 'a beggar was pointed out to me. An Islamic tradition ascribes to King Solomon a signet ring that allowed him to understand the language of the birds. Everyone knew that the beggar had this ring in his possession. It was of such inestimable value that he could never sell it, and he died in one of the courtyards of the mosque of Wazir Khan, in Lahore.'

I reflected that Chaucer was not unaware of the legend of the extraordinary ring, but to have said so would have spoiled Barclay's anecdote.

'And the signet ring?' I asked.

'It was lost, as is the inevitable fate of magical objects. Perhaps it's still there now in some nook of the mosque or on the hand of some man who lives in a place where there are no birds.'

'Or where there are so many,' I said, 'that what they say is confused.'

It was then that Daniel Thorpe spoke up. He did so in an impersonal way, without looking at us. 'Your story has something of the parable about it, Barclay.' His pronunciation was a bit strange, and I attributed this to his long residence in the East. 'But it's not a parable,' he said, 'or if it is, it's nonetheless true. There are things of such inestimable value that they can't be sold.'

The words that I am trying now to piece together impressed me less than the conviction with which Daniel Thorpe uttered them. We thought he would say something more, but all at once he fell silent, as if he regretted having spoken. Barclay said goodbye. Thorpe and I made our way back to our hotel together. By now it was quite late, but Thorpe suggested that we carry on our talk in his room.

After one or two inconsequential remarks, he said, 'I offer you the king's signet ring. Of course, we are using a metaphor, but what this metaphor comprises is no less prodigious than the ring. I offer you Shakespeare's memory from his youngest (and oldest) days down to early April, 1616.'

I could not utter a single word. It was as if I had been offered the sea.

'I am not an impostor,' Thorpe went on. 'I am not mad. I beg you to suspend judgment until you have heard me out. The major probably told you that I am – or was – an army doctor. The story requires few words. It begins in the East, in a gore-stained hospital, as dawn was breaking. The exact date is of no importance. A common soldier, Adam Clay, had been hit by two rifle bullets. Just before his end, with his last breath, he offered me the precious memory. Fever and the throes of death are both inventive states; I accepted the offer without really believing in it. Besides, after a battle, nothing is strange. Clay barely had time to explain the singular conditions of the gift. The giver has to offer it and the receiver accept it aloud. He who gives it loses it forever.'

The soldier's name and the emotional scene seemed to me literary in the bad sense of the word.

'You have Shakespeare's memory now?' I asked, slightly intimidated.

'I still have two memories,' Thorpe answered. 'My own memory and Shakespeare's, who, in part, I am. In other words, two memories possess me. There is an area where they overlap. There is a woman's face that I am not sure in which century to place.'

'What have you done with Shakespeare's memory?' I asked.

There was silence, and then he said, 'I have written a fictionalized biography that earned the critics' scorn and some commercial success in the United States and in the colonies. I believe that is all. I have forewarned you that my gift is not a sinecure. I still await your answer.'

I kept turning it over in my mind. Had I not devoted my life, a life which had been as colourless as it had been strange, to the search for Shakespeare? Wasn't it only fair that at the end of the day I should meet him?

'I accept Shakespeare's memory,' I said, enunciating each word clearly.

No doubt something happened, but I did not feel it. The merest touch of weariness – possibly imagined.

'The memory has now entered into your consciousness,' I distinctly remember Thorpe saying, 'but you have to discover it. It will arise in your dreams or while you are awake, turning the pages of a book perhaps or rounding a street corner. Don't be impatient; don't make up any memories. Chance may favour it or delay it, according to its mysterious way. As I begin to forget, you will remember. I cannot give you a date.'

We spent what remained of the night arguing about

Shylock's character. I refrained from trying to find out whether Shakespeare had had any personal dealings with Jews. I did not want Thorpe to think that I was putting him to a test. I confirmed, I don't know whether with relief or uneasiness, that his opinions were as academic and conventional as my own.

In spite of my late hours the night before, that night I barely slept. I discovered, as on so many other occasions, that I was a coward. Fearing disappointment, I did not give in to generous hope. I wanted to think that Thorpe's gift was an illusion. Irresistibly, hope prevailed. Shakespeare would be mine as no one had ever been anyone else's, either in love or friendship or even hate. Somehow, I would be Shakespeare. I would not write the tragedies or the complex sonnets, but I would remember the moment when the witches, who are also the Fates, were revealed to me and that other moment, when I was given the vast lines,

And shake the yoke of inauspicious stars
From this world-weary flesh.

I was to remember Anne Hathaway as I recall that woman, now in her maturity, who taught me love in an apartment in Lübeck so many years ago. (I tried to remember her but could only recall the wallpaper, which was yellow, and the light that came in from the window. This first calamity ought to have prepared me for the others.) I had assumed that the images of my prodigious memory would, first and foremost, be visual. The reality was otherwise. Days later, while shaving, I found myself pronouncing into the mirror words that were strange to me and that belonged, as a colleague pointed out, to the language of Chaucer. One afternoon, as I left the British Museum, I began to whistle a very simple tune that I had never heard before.

By now the reader will have noticed the characteristic common to the first revelations of a memory which was, in spite of the splendour of a handful of metaphors, rather more auditory than visual.

De Quincey holds that the brain is a palimpsest. Each new thing written on it covers the previous and in turn is covered by the next, but omnipotent memory may exhume any impression, no matter how fleeting it may have been, if given sufficient stimulus. To judge by Shakespeare's testament, there was not a single book – not even a Bible – in his house, but everyone knows the works he consulted: Chaucer, Gower, Spenser, Christopher Marlowe, Holinshed's *Chronicles*, Florio's Montaigne, North's Plutarch. I was in possession of Shakespeare's memory in a latent way; the reading – that is, the re-reading – of those old volumes would provide the stimulus I sought. I re-read the sonnets, which are his most immediate work. Once or twice I came up with an explanation or various explanations. Good verse demands reading aloud; after a few days, I effortlessly recovered the harsh r's and open vowels of the sixteenth century.

I wrote in the *Zeitschrift für germanische Philologie* that Sonnet 127 referred to the memorable defeat of the Spanish Armada. I did not remember that in 1899 Samuel Butler had already formulated this thesis.

A visit to Stratford-on-Avon, foreseeably, was fruitless. After that, I detected the gradual transformation of my dreams. They were not furnished, as were De Quincey's, with splendid nightmares or with pious allegorical visions in the manner of his master, Jean Paul. Faces and unfamiliar rooms entered my nights. The first face I identified was Chapman's; then Ben Jonson's and a neighbour of his who does not figure in the biographies but whom Shakespeare often saw.

Anyone acquiring an encyclopedia does not acquire each line, each paragraph, each page, or each engraving; he acquires the mere possibility of becoming familiar with some of these. If this happens with a relatively simple, concrete entity, given the alphabetical order of its parts, what may not happen with an abstract, random entity, *ondoyant et divers*, like the magic memory of a dead man?

To no one is it granted to embrace in a single moment the fullness of his past. Neither Shakespeare, as far as I know, nor I, his partial inheritor, were given this gift. A man's memory is not a sum; it is a disorder of undefined possibilities. Saint Augustine, if I am not mistaken, speaks of the palaces and caverns of memory. The second metaphor is more apt. It was into these caverns that I entered.

Like our own, Shakespeare's memory included areas, great shadowy areas, deliberately rejected by him. With a certain shame, I remembered that Ben Jonson made him recite Greek and Latin hexameters and that Shakespeare's ear, his incomparable ear, would stumble over a quantity amid the boisterous laughter of his cronies.

I knew states of happiness and gloom that transcend the common experience of mankind. Without my being aware of it, long studious solitude had prepared me to receive the miracle passively.

After some thirty days, the dead man's memory came alive in me. During the course of a week of strange happiness, I almost believed I was Shakespeare. His work took on new life. I know that for Shakespeare the moon was not so much the moon as Diana and not so much Diana as that slow-sounding, slow-moving word – 'moon'. I made another discovery. Shakespeare's apparent mistakes, those '*absences dans l'infini*' of which Hugo speaks apologetically, were deliberate.

Shakespeare overlooked them, or introduced them, so
that his speech, as it was destined for the stage, would
seem spontaneous and not too polished or contrived
(*nicht allzu glatt und gekünstelt*). This same reason
prompted him to mix his metaphors:

> my way of life
> Is fall'n into the sear, the yellow leaf.

One day I detected a guilty secret deep in his
memory. I did not try to pinpoint it; Shakespeare
already has for all time. Let me only say that this guilt
had nothing to do with perversion.

I realised that the three faculties of the human soul –
memory, understanding, and will – are not a scholastic
fiction. Shakespeare's memory was unable to reveal
anything other than facts. It is obvious that such facts
do not constitute Shakespeare's uniqueness; what mat-
ters is the work that he created with that perishable
matter.

Naïvely, like Thorpe, I had envisaged a biography. I
soon found out that that genre requires of a writer
qualifications that certainly are not mine. I have no skill
at narration. I have no skill at narrating my own
history, which is somewhat more unusual than Shakespeare's. Besides, such a book would be pointless.
Chance or fate gave Shakespeare the trivial things, the
terrible things that every man experiences; he knew
how to turn them into fables, into characters much
more vivid than the grey man who dreamed them up,
into lines that generations will go on reading, into word
music. Why unweave that net, why undermine the
tower, why reduce the sound and fury of *Macbeth* to
the convenient size of a documented biography or a re-
alistic novel?

As everyone knows, Goethe functions as the official

cult of Germany; more intimate to us Germans is the cult of Shakespeare, which we profess not without nostalgia. (In England, Shakespeare, who is so far distant from the English, functions as the official cult; the book of England is the Bible.)

In the first stages of the adventure I felt the happiness of being Shakespeare; in the last, the oppression and terror. At the outset the two memories did not mingle their waters, but in time Shakespeare's great river threatened and almost swamped my modest trickle. I noticed with misgivings that I was losing my fathers' tongue. Since one's own identity is based on memory, I feared for my reason.

My friends paid me visits; it astonished me that they did not perceive that I was in hell. I began not to understand the everyday world about me (*die alltägliche Umwelt*). One particular morning I lost myself among great shapes of iron, wood, and glass, bewildered by hissing sounds and a great din. For a moment, which to me seemed infinite, I was unable to recognize the engines and coaches of Bremen station.

In relation to the passing years, each of us is obliged to bear the growing burden of his memory. Two memories weighed me down, mine and the other man's, sometimes mingling but mutually incommunicable.

All things try to keep on being themselves, Spinoza tells us. A stone wants to be a stone, the tiger a tiger; I wanted to be Hermann Soergel again.

I have forgotten the date I made up my mind to free myself. I hit upon the easiest way, dialling telephone numbers at random. I got children's or women's voices. I considered it my duty to respect them. Finally, I chanced upon a cultured male voice.

'Would you like Shakespeare's memory?' I said. 'I know what I am offering you is very serious. Think it over.'

'I shall take that risk,' an incredulous voice answered. 'I accept Shakespeare's memory.'

I stated the conditions of the gift. Paradoxically, at one and the same time I felt nostalgia for the book I ought to have written but that was forbidden me to write and the fear that my guest, the ghost, would never leave me.

I replaced the receiver and repeated like a prayer these words of recognition: 'Simply the thing I am shall make me live.'

I had contrived disciplines to awaken old memories; now I had to seek others to erase them. One of the many was the study of the mythology of William Blake, that unruly disciple of Swedenborg. I found out that Blake was less complex than complicated.

That and other paths proved useless; all led me back to Shakespeare. In the end, I came upon the only solution to flesh out my hopes – the strict, vast music of Bach.

P.S. 1924 – Now I am a man like other men. In my waking hours I am Professor Emeritus Hermann Soergel, who once played with a card catalog and compiled learned trivialities, but sometimes as the day dawns I am aware that the one who sleeps is the other man. Now and again, I am surprised by fleeting snatches of memory that may be real.

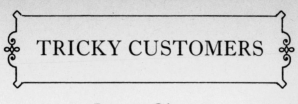

TRICKY CUSTOMERS

James Chatto

There is something about a good bookshop that lures eccentrics; it beckons and draws them as a conjuror does children, offering enchanted diversion. When the bookshop is small and erudite its attraction is doubled, and if it should also happen to be located in a part of London with a large resident lunatic fringe, as was the place where I once worked, the patronage of the socially abnormal can amount to infestation.

We were called Michael Adam Ltd and we occupied an old two-storey building, with low, sagging ceilings and a big display window, in a backstreet between Fulham and Knightsbridge. The premises were too small, really, for the enormous variety of our stock, but they contributed to the tranquil, dusty atmosphere that our clientele found so tempting. Downstairs we kept the books that sold, the new biographies, fiction, art and history, atlases, cooking and travel; upstairs, crowded by the paperbacks, were the more arcane categories: philosophy, religion, the occult, musicology, antiques, crafts and poetry. The majority of our customers, people who actually wanted to buy a book, rarely climbed the narrow stairs into this den, but the eccentrics made a beeline for it. Solitary figures, they came to browse, resenting any intrusion, some using the room like a library, most just seeking sanctuary from the bustle walking in off the streets for an hour or so as people used to into a church.

At least, that is what I reckoned during my first few days in the job: I put our popularity down to the ambience, but it soon became clear that the real reason

had much more to do with my employer, Michael
Adam, a man of charm and infallible literary expertise,
with the most beautiful manners in the world. Difficult
old ladies melted at his smile; furious women with
twenty carrier bags and a parking ticket were soothed
within minutes by his subtly distracting small talk.
When I tried to imitate him I became merely obsequi-
ous or cheeky, but Michael had the ability to delight
them without even trying. He made foolish people
seem clever, giving them things to say about the latest
fashionable *Collected Letters*; and clever people
listened attentively to his more profound opinions,
expressed so casually that no one ever felt challenged by
his knowledge. The secret, I suppose, was his endless
patience, and the fact that he genuinely liked his fellow
man as much as he liked books, and enjoyed bringing
the two together.

That he prospered as a result did not displease him.
He made a reasonable living from the wealthy gentry
who shopped and gossipped downstairs, and they
enjoyed the sight of the odd Bohemian as he edged past
the shelves towards the staircase, feeling themselves in
touch with the poetical and the avant-garde. As for the
eccentrics themselves, they idolised Michael, sharing
with him the grievances and triumphs of their peculiar
little worlds. They would have defended our shop with
their lives, and all because he took them seriously.

He was even kind to Senor Petche. The Senor was
one of our dottier regulars and to me his habits were
deeply irritating. At six o'clock, just as we were closing,
his wrinkled, monkey head would loom out of the darkness and peer in hopelessly through the window. Sometimes I pretended to ignore him, but more often we
would sigh and gather smiles from our tired faces and
turn the lights back on upstairs. Then he would come
in, bobbing a bow, a hesitant grin trembling on his thin

ascetic lips. He always wore black – a suit and tie and a trim overcoat with an astrakhan collar, and black leather gloves that clutched a miniature umbrella. Dapper, wistful and five feet tall, he would hover by the door until Michael went forward to greet him.

It was no good my feigning a welcome. Whenever I spoke to him he looked away and stepped back surreptitiously, whispering something in his querulous, accented falsetto, too quietly for me to hear. Only Michael could penetrate his acute shyness and over the years he had refined this manoeuvre to an art. While Senor Petche darted agonised glances at me, Michael drew his attention inexorably into the twin securities of his pet subjects, bibliography and metaphysics. It was like trying to light a fire with damp straw, but sooner or later the smoke began to rise. My presence was forgotten, as was the rest of the world, and Senor Petche would lay down his umbrella, lick his lips and frown down at some title page, his chin lifted to the light.

'He's rather good on Jung,' Michael might suggest. A small apologetic cough from the Senor, perhaps the echo of a coy giggle.

'Yes, indeed, largely, indeed, but you know I heard him lecture in Prague in 1959 and you will forgive me Michael but he showed so small an understanding of the Jungian interest in alchemy that one is permitted to wonder . . .' And he was off.

How Petche coped outside the shop is a mystery. His nerves discouraged him from going out until dusk, but I gathered from overheard remarks that his own library was extensive and no doubt he could function there. Among books he suddenly became cool and self-assured, even masterful; beyond them he was nothing. I think Michael was his only friend – confessor, Samaritan, confidant – as he was to so many others.

Then, in the early spring of 1983, we were blessed

with the patronage of another, very different bizarre.

It was a cold, bright morning and I was busy unpacking orders in the tiny office at the back of the shop when I heard the bell on the door. I looked through the spyhole but could see no one. Turning back, I nearly touched a man who was suddenly standing behind me. He was obviously delighted at my terrified start and his handsome face – Errol Flynn with a hint of Charles the Second – broke into a grin.

'Is Michael here?' he purred.

I explained that he had gone out for a moment but would soon be back.

'I'll wait upstairs.'

He disappeared up to the den and I breathed again. Even if he hadn't scared me like that I think his appearance would have proved affecting. It was calculated to be so. He must have been six foot six, in his forties and clearly very fit, and he wore a floor-length brown kaftan with a Russian collar, drawn in at the waist by a monk's cord, and heavy riding boots. Hearing him clump about upstairs I wondered how on earth he had moved so silently and so fast from the shop door to the office. And there was a smell in the air, very faint, of patchouli.

When Michael came in I told him there was someone to see him and he called out a cheerful hello. We heard an answering 'Ah!' and the footsteps crossing the room and then the kaftan appeared. Beside me Michael inhaled sharply. I looked round at him. His calm, urbane face was scowling. Then our customer's head ducked under the arch of the staircase and Michael managed to assume his usual expression.

'Hello Michael,' drawled Kaftan. 'I gave your boy here a bit of a turn. How are you? Coining it?'

'Not bad . . .'

Kaftan had turned away without waiting for an

answer. 'Same old crap on your shelves. Don't suppose you've anything for me.'

'Probably not.'

I found it hard not to stare at Michael. I had never heard him so cold. Kaftan picked up a book from the central display, glanced at it and dropped it back onto the pile. Then he sniffed, grotesquely, as if he were taking snuff.

'I'll dictate a list of books for you to get for me,' he said. 'Fetch a pen, Bunter.'

I tried to look haughty as I obeyed him, but I was unconvincing. The list was long and consisted of ponderous titles to do with magic and natural philosophy. I recognized none of them.

Michael had stood to one side as I wrote. 'I'll drop you a card if we can find any,' he said.

'No. I'll be in and out. I'm staying in town for a couple of months.' The man's eyes wandered briefly round the shop, his mouth set in a sneer. Then he suddenly stared at me. 'Boo!' he shouted, and with a swish of his robe he strode out into the street and away.

'God! Who was that?'

Michael looked troubled. 'That was Major Jonathan Galloway. He used to come in here a lot, once upon a time.'

'Does he always wear that outfit?'

'Mmm.'

'What does he do?'

Michael was looking at the list glumly. He glanced up. 'What? Sorry?'

'I wondered what he does?'

He shrugged. 'I really don't know. I've known him for years. He went to my school in fact. He was a vindictive little chap in those days. And about ten years ago he ruined someone I was very fond of. Nothing was proved but he did it all right.' He paused by the office entrance. 'He told me once he was a warlock.'

Major Galloway returned a week later. Michael and I were both busy with Lady N, helping her decide what to give her many friends for Easter and trying to stop her dachshunds from peeing on the stock. Whether he saw the dogs or not I do not know, but as he strode through us, the Major contrived to punt one of them clear across the floor, into the side of the box where we keep the Michelin guides. Lady N screamed, as did the dachshund – the other one started to scamper about yapping – and somehow a pile of books slipped off a table. Major Galloway just stamped upstairs. A moment later we heard him laughing.

Michael calmed Lady N down while she keened over her hysterical but undamaged dog. I carried her books out to her car. As she drove away she shot me a look of profound reproach.

When I got back to the shop Galloway was downstairs again, and apparently in an ugly mood.

We had done our best with his list, but if a book is out of print there is little that a shop like ours, selling only new publications, can do to acquire it. All but two of Galloway's were no longer available, and those two had to be ordered from the States.

He swung round as I came in.

'I suppose you set this oaf on the job,' he said. The sneer I had noticed before was back. 'Really Michael, there's more to running a bookshop than pimping memoirs to the parish dowagers. If my requirements are too high-brow you should have said so instead of wasting my time. The only reason I came here at all was because of the old connection.'

Michael's lips were dry and pulled back from his teeth. He paused for a moment before responding.

'The things you asked for are all rather obscure – obviously you know that. I'll get you the two I can and, if you like, I'll put an advertisement in *The Clique* for the others.'

'That I could have done for myself!'

'Yup. Well I think you should. Or there are other shops specialising . . .'

'I am aware of the other shops!'

'Well perhaps you'd be better off looking there?'

'Or perhaps you could pull your thumb out a bit, eh? Do it yourself instead of palming the work off on your help.'

Michael smiled. 'There's nothing I could do that James didn't.'

'I dare say.'

'Really, I think you should try the occult bookshops.'

'Oh you do.' He exhaled noisily. 'Look. You've got a week. I can't wait for ever.'

'No, you don't understand. What I'm saying is I don't want your custom.'

Galloway narrowed his eyes and stared. 'Say again?'

'I don't want your custom.'

The Major let it sink in, then he suddenly threw back his head and roared with laughter. It was a harsh, mirthless noise, so loud that it hurt my ears.

'You don't want my custom! You stupid little man.' He took a step towards Michael, towering over him, fists balled and white-knuckled. 'You stupid little bastard. Don't you dare try and tell me where I can or can't shop!'

I was cringing, sick and useless, but somehow Michael kept his ground and his temper.

'Get out,' he said quietly.

I was sure Galloway was going to hit him, but he didn't. Instead he just stood there, his muscles so tense that he seemed to quiver, his breathing clearly audible. He appeared to be having some sort of apoplectic fit. The veins at his temples throbbed and his eyes bulged, unfocused – the room was full of his anger. It was stifling, an almost tangible pressure. And then the whole world exploded... Well, not the world of course, but the enormous plate glass windows of the shop. There was an actual detonation and the air was suddenly lethal with showering glass. I threw myself down onto the floor while razor-sharp debris crashed about me and I am sure I heard the Major mutter *Damn You* as he swept past. When I looked up he was gone.

Michael clambered slowly to his feet. There was glass everywhere, even in our clothes. Splinters had cut our faces and hands and another shard had torn my trousers at the knee and cut me there. Blades of the stuff stuck out of books, embedded in their spines and jackets; the display in the window was ruined. The traffic up on the Brompton Road seemed very loud.

Michael is a methodical man. I wanted to stand and gape and discuss what had happened there and then, but he made it clear as we bandaged our wounds from the first aid kit in the office that the shop must come before my curiosity. So while I swept up the wreckage and moved lacerated stock down into the basement he phoned about for a glazier capable of repairing our window that afternoon. It was not until work was under way, just after three, that he showed any signs of relaxing.

'It was magic, wasn't it,' was my proposition. Michael shrugged wearily, but I persisted. 'Mind over matter. A psychic blow. That's what magic means isn't it: material change wrought by mental energies?'

'You could say the same about an influential book.'

'How did he do it, though?'

'Honestly, I haven't the faintest idea.'

'And what exactly did he do?'

Michael was staring at me. The elastoplast on his

nose gave him an irritable look.

'I don't think either of us are even qualified to guess, James, do you? Why not take the afternoon off. I'll stay and see to the work.'

'Well okay, if you're sure ... Thanks! He really is a warlock, though, wouldn't you say? I mean he really is.'

I did not expect to see Major Galloway again, but a week later to the day, he breezed in in his chocolate-coloured kaftan and stood before me, grinning. Michael was out at lunch and there was no one else in the shop. It occurred to me that I ought to tell him to leave, but I decided against it. He just stood there, enjoying my discomfiture. Then a piece of paper fluttered from his hand, coming to rest on a boxed set of the new Proust.

'Settling my account,' he said. He widened his eyes dramatically and turned to go. 'And I shall continue to do business here,' he added at the door.

The paper was a cheque for five hundred pounds.

Michael scowled when he returned and I told him what had happened. He asked me to look at the credit book and nodded when I reported that the Major had no debts to his name. I took the book back into the office. When I came back, Michael had torn up the cheque and dropped it into the bin. Later I heard him typing – a letter to Galloway, telling him to keep his distance.

For weeks after that a sort of gloom hung over us. We both believed that the warlock would return for a confrontation, not wanting to leave the last word with us. As dusk fell each evening and he still had not arrived our relief was enormous, but each morning resharpened the Damoclean sword. The last thing I wanted was to have to delay our locking-up at night, therefore, but I had forgotten the habits of the other loonie, Senor Petche. One Wednesday evening, prompt as ever at six, he materialised in the twilight, scratching at the new window like Cathy's ghost.

Michael let him in. In a way he was something of a tonic, with his whispered gratitude and harmless self-absorption, darting shy affection at Michael. For the first time I felt myself warming to him and perhaps he detected it, for I was suddenly included in the conversation.

Michael had been telling him about Galloway's exhibition and he was keenly aroused by the story, nodding and frowning at each detail. I was listening at a distance great enough to avoid worrying him, when he turned and looked up at me.

'You also were abused?' he piped, with a little moue of sympathy.

'Yes I was!'

'But you heard no actual incantation. He fumed in silence.'

'He just stood there.'

'And then the window . . . I see. How very interesting. Such power. I would like to meet this warlock of yours.' He began to murmur about poltergeists, blinking rapidly, then his head twitched. 'There is something pertinent, as it happens, in one of the books upstairs. May I fetch it?'

'Of course.'

'One wonders about the extent of the control a man of his temper could exert over the subtle energies . . .' He peered at Michael. 'But here I am hypothesising over what is to you a very personal predicament. Forgive me. I am distressed and may I say enraged by such treatment of a friend.' He dithered, wishing, I think, to say more, and then remembered the book upstairs. 'Two minutes!'

As the old man climbed out of sight I made a face at Michael. He smiled, looking down at his watch.

'God. You might as well go home.'

'Are you sure?'

'Yup. Go on.'

Well it was already past time. I went into the office for my coat. The light in there was off but enough spilled in from the shop for me to see Major Galloway, motionless, impossibly tall, pressed against the wall in the deep shadows. His eyes were open and he was leering down at me.

I made a sort of strangled whimper and the skin on my head and neck prickled with terror. His eyes rolled insanely and returned to mine. I started to shiver, dumb and rooted. Then I heard Michael's voice: 'Hang on for a second will you, James, I'm just going to bring the car round.' I heard the shop door open and close, I heard my heart pounding, and then, like a clarion of heaven, a tiny cough from upstairs – Senor Petche reminding us that he was still there.

A hiss escaped the Major. Very slowly, his gaze never wavering, he detached himself from the wall.

'I shall finish what I began,' he muttered.

He stepped out into the light of the shop, gliding towards the staircase. To my shame, I did nothing. I didn't even move. The darkness in the office was a blanket to hide under. His boots were heavy on the stairs, on the floorboards above.

Only then did I creep a little way, just to the archway of the office, still half in shadow. I heard Galloway speak.

'You were asking after me, sir.'

Something inaudible from Senor Petche... I edged a pace closer to the bottom of the stairs.

'And on what do you base this presumption?'

More murmuring.

'I do as I please! I was insulted in this place and I shall enjoy my revenge.'

[43]

Then I heard Senor Petche. He was asking Galloway to leave his friend alone.

'Are you threatening me?' boomed the Major. 'Are you? Very well then.'

Petche spoke again, again too softly for me to catch a word. There was a terrible peel of laughter, like the braying of a mule. And then silence.

I should have gone up. I wanted to run away. But that awful silence precluded any movement. Once I thought I heard a tiny creak, like a riding boot or a shoe, but it could have been my own taut neck. When the bell on the door went ping I felt as though I'd been punched in the stomach.

It was Michael. He looked tired and started to apologise for keeping me waiting. Then he noticed my expression.

'He's up there,' I croaked, 'With Petche.'

Michael winced as if in pain, but he did not hesitate. His foot was already on the bottom step when the Senor appeared above him. We both fell back.

Senor Petche was smiling, almost glowing. His descent was superb in its dignity. Neither of us said a thing.

'I took the liberty of introducing myself to your friend,' he murmured demurely, when he had joined us. 'And of criticising his manners.'

I was staring past him up the stairs.

'Major Galloway is no longer up there. I was correct about that book, Michael, and my consultation of it was, in fact, rather timely. However I already possess a copy. I would like to buy this instead. It does not appear to be priced.'

He held out a book. It was heavy and large and bound in chocolate-coloured cloth.

I reached out automatically, but Michael put a hand on my arm.

'Please take it as a gift.'

Senor Petche smiled again. 'Thank you. It will fill a gap in my collection. A work of vigour and some style, but without any real sense of direction.'

'What did you do?' I asked, unable to bear it any longer. The Senor looked decidedly embarrassed. He seemed to be searching for words.

'Bibliopegy?' he suggested at last. 'You see, I take issue with the adage: a book usually can be judged by its binding.'

He said goodnight and left, his new volume under his arm.

A little later Michael and I went upstairs. There was no sign of a struggle, nothing strange at all. We tidied the stacks for a while in silence. It was only when I finally turned to follow Michael down that I thought I detected something – just the merest hint of patchouli in the air. The fancy lingered for weeks.

ALL LIVING THINGS

Clare Colvin

The house stood on its own among fields of young wheat, reached by an unmetalled road that ran past one side and on towards the horizon. When the wind stirred through the fields they became a sea of shimmering green silk, with the house marooned in the middle, keeping the waves at bay with an indeterminate hedge. It had once been two cottages for farmworkers' families, but for the last year it had been empty. People did not like living in isolation now, except for the few who searched it out.

'Not another house for miles and miles around, just fields and sky and silence!' Deborah turned to Frank, her eyes shining with the vision of space. She put her arm through his, and rubbed her face against his shoulder. Frank's eyes were more sharply focussed. He saw the slates missing from the roof, the peeling paint of the window frames, the lichen on the paving stones by the back door, but he saw, too, the solidity of the flint and brick walls, built to withstand the winds sweeping across the land from the North Sea. He disentangled his arm from hers and walked towards the house, with a proprietorial air, to prod at the wood of the window frames with the house keys.

'A couple of coats of creosote should fix that. It's all in good nick outside. I don't think we'll have any trouble once we've done the roof and the damp course.'

Deborah was not listening. She was gazing at the fields that stretched into the distance and at the marestail clouds high overhead. From a nearby apple tree a thrush made a contented gurgling sound, echoing

[49]

the satisfaction in her soul.

'Not another house for miles around, just fields of waving corn stretching as far as the eye can see!' Deborah's face was flushed with the effects of wine as well as elation as she sat at Nick and Nina's dinner table, describing her vision.

'But Deborah, you do realise they come and *cut* the corn?' asked Nina. 'You realise that in winter you will be surrounded by miles and miles of *mud*?'

'That's the way it should be,' said Deborah, undeterred. 'The changing seasons... In town we're hardly aware of the time of year. We're both beginning to feel there's a lack of life here. We live in a house with a tiny backyard, with two tubs of flowers and one lonely little rabbit in a hutch. In the country we'll be able to have rabbits and chickens, maybe a goat. We've had this feeling for some time that the way we live now isn't right for us any more.'

'Your rabbits and chickens will, of course, be slaughtered by the local foxes, but that's all part of nature's rich pattern,' said Nick. 'Have some more of this delicious mousse aux deux chocolats which Nina discovered in the Haverstock Deli and remember it when you're cutting the weevils out of your windfalls to make an apple pie. What about you, Frank? Why are you chasing this idyll in the country? I always thought you were a town boy.'

The term 'town boy', coming from Nick, public school and Oxford, was not lost on Frank. He realised Deborah's friends found their marriage incongruous. They would not have met in the first place had the magazine Deborah worked for not been printed by the firm where Frank had been a rep. Deborah, the daughter of home counties wealth, and Frank, from the meaner streets of Hackney.

'Make sure you get what you want in this life,

because otherwise they'll take away what little you already have,' his father had said. It was an uneasy home, where you were never sure what might set off an explosion of temper, and Frank's mother was quiet and sad, aware that whatever she once had must have been taken away. He remembered the holidays with his uncle in Essex. They would walk through the fields, his uncle striding ahead, carrying his gun, Frank following behind with the canvas bag for the rabbits. Those were times of escape and freedom, and the house in Suffolk offered another escape, freedom to be himself, not to be judged by people like Nick and Nina. The job of managing the firm in Ipswich had come at the right moment. He knew that he and Deborah had lost the closeness they used to have, but he also knew that the receptions, the first nights, the film previews, all those little events that media people cossetted themselves with to keep the real world at bay, did not satisfy her.

'You know *Essex*, do you?' said Nick. 'That's another very flat place. Not that I've been there. No doubt we'll find our way to Suffolk *if* the weather gets extremely hot. Nina, dear, do stop hugging the port to yourself and pass it around. Frank's glass is empty again.'

There is a certain sadness in seeing a house you once filled with your furniture, which you built up into your own outer shell, stripped of its possessions, leaving only the detritus that gathers under furniture and marks on the walls where once there were mirrors and pictures. Deborah wandered around the empty house for a last imprint on her memory. There was the sitting room with its stripped pine floor where they had held so many parties, beginning in the early days with wine and French bread and cheese, and graduating to buffets of chili con carne or a whole salmon. Upstairs, the sun slanted through the sash windows in the room where

[51]

she had spent her first night with Frank. They had gone to a film together and afterwards she had invited him in for coffee, not with any particular intent, but he looked lonely on the doorstep and she did not want the evening to end just then. She had sat on the sofa, and he in the chair by the fireplace, and she wanted to reach out and touch his face, but would not for the world confess it. Almost as if he had guessed, he got up from his chair and knelt before her, his arms drawing her towards him, and said, 'I want to go to bed with you more than I want anything in the world . . . but only if you want me to . . .' Such a simple want, so easily satisfied, but from it came a succession of other wants – to be together more, to have a relationship that meant as much to both of them, to be married. He was never really happy in that house. It had been bought for her by her parents, and each piece of furniture carried with it memories of weekends spent in the junk shops of seaside towns, in the days before Frank. They needed a home of shared, equal memories, somewhere they could build together.

The furniture van was loaded with its final item – Peter Rabbit in his hutch – and Deborah turned the key in the front door for the last time, before they drove to the estate agent.

'Ten years of my life handed to a spotty-faced young man I don't particularly like,' she said to Frank as she returned to the car.

'It could be worse. Some women can say that about their husbands,' he said, his eyes looking at her with that flash of blue that somehow made everything all right, and which in the last year or so had been far rarer. She felt relieved for she had, in the final tension of moving, wondered if she was not, after all, making a terrible mistake.

That first morning in June, Deborah opened the

door, stepped into the garden, and saw spread out before her, like a gift, the open countryside – clean-washed by the overnight dew, with gentle swirls of mist over the fields. She felt triumphant, for this land was hers to look at every day for years ahead. She walked down the indistinct gravel path, past the tufted grass that was once a lawn, where Peter Rabbit's hutch was now placed, past the apple trees and a garden shed to a privet hedge behind which were the remains of a compost heap and remnants of the previous inhabitants – a rusted enamel bowl, an empty gas cylinder and a broken pushchair.

She stood on the garden's edge and watched the cloud shadows moving across the fields. Her ears could hear every sound for miles around, a tractor somewhere in the distance, the sigh of the green wheat as it bowed almost imperceptibly to a breeze. As she stood there, her senses sharpened, watching everything, she was aware of herself being watched. On the bank that separated the field from the road, a large black cat, frozen in the moment of stillness before flight, was staring at her. Its eyes were exactly the colour of the grass and for a moment she felt she was looking through a black silhouette at the ground behind it.

'Come here,' she said. 'Puss, puss...' As she extended her hand towards the cat, it turned and cut swiftly through the undergrowth.

After breakfast, Deborah and Frank walked along the straight track that ran past their house through the fields. Fifty yards ahead of them a pheasant strutted across the road and into the hedgerow.

'I'm going to buy a gun next time I go to Bury St Edmunds,' said Frank. 'These birds are practically given away on a plate.'

'You can't shoot pheasants, they belong to whoever owns the land,' said Deborah. 'You can't shoot them until October anyway, and you certainly can't shoot them when they are walking across the road. It's not considered fair.'

'Since when has there been a law against being unfair?' asked Frank. 'No one would know whether I was shooting pheasants or rabbits.'

'Not rabbits, either,' said Deborah. 'They're all relations of Peter's.'

'Stop behaving like Beatrix Potter, girl. This is the real countryside. The animals here eat the crops, and then they get killed and eaten. That's the natural law. My aunt used to make great rabbit pies after we'd been out hunting. There's nothing like them.'

Frank bought a gun a few weeks later in Bury St Edmunds and had it licensed. He sat dismantling and re-assembling it beside the newly installed Aga while Deborah peeled apples at the kitchen table. This, she thought, was what their life here was supposed to be, but she did not feel satisfied by it. The closeness that should have come from being together and working on the cottage was elusive. Frank talked less now and often his conversation took the form of orders. Have you done this? Do that. Why didn't you do it this way?

When they had given up what had become two almost independent lives in a shared house, they had not considered that, in different circumstances, their reactions to each other might change. Deborah was now working only two days a week at the magazine, but Frank had a much better paid and more responsible job in Ipswich. He was beginning to absorb other views, other attitudes from the people he worked with. Clearly in her head, Deborah heard the words 'reverting to type' and, to break her chain of thought, she said inconsequentially the first thing that came to her, 'We must look like a pioneer couple – you cleaning a gun and me making apple pie.'

'We're no different from any other couple, not the ones *I* know anyway,' said Frank, picking up a newspaper. 'When are we going to eat?'

Deborah went into the garden, partly in order not to reply, and partly to see to Peter Rabbit. He seemed agitated. His nose twitched rapidly and his eyes were startled and staring in the direction of the apple trees. She looked towards the nearest one and there it was again, the steady green gaze of the cat. They both froze for a moment, then as Deborah moved forward, the cat disappeared through the hedge and across the road.

'What the hell is this saucer of milk doing here?' demanded Frank, a few days later, after he had tipped it over with his feet outside the backdoor.

'It's that black cat I told you about. I've seen it skulking about the garden looking hungry, and I was trying to feed it,' said Deborah.

'It's a wild cat, Deb, it's feral. It catches mice and rats and rabbits. It doesn't know what saucers of milk are about.'

'Rabbits...' Deborah saw Peter Rabbit, whom she had let out of his hutch, twitching his nose amongst clumps of grass.

'It's probably after Peter. You should scare it off, not leave offerings around for it.'

That evening as they were companionably intertwined on the sofa watching television, there was a sound outside of metal hitting the ground. The dustbin lid lay rocking on its handle, and the paper which had earlier been wrapped round the meat was torn and scattered on the ground. A black shadow slid away through the hedge.

Frank turned angrily on Deborah. 'That's what comes of encouraging it. You can never tame them once they've turned wild. You'll only make it bolder.' His emotion seemed out of proportion to the event, as if the cat was a threatened invasion.

Later that night, in bed, Deborah reached out her hand and touched Frank's face. Whatever happened during the day, there were moments when she knew they were perfectly right to have come here, to be alone, away from the world, re-learning their life together. She had stopped taking the pill as soon as they left London, and now, in their cottage among the fields, each time they made love might be the time they made a baby, a new life for them both. Afterwards Frank's hand would rest on her stomach, sending warmth to an incipient being within.

'I had lunch with Deborah yesterday, and she was absolutely vibrating with expectancy,' said Nina to Nick as they took their wire basket around the Haverstock Deli.

'I knew she'd turn fecund as soon as they were among their fields of turnips,' said Nick.

'Fields of wheat, much more attractive. Look, they've got tripes à la mode as a made-up dish. Shall we have some for tonight? And carrottes rapées to start with?'

'Wouldn't it be cheaper to buy them from the greengrocer and do them yourself?' said Nick.

'I'm not grating carrot after carrot after carrot. We'll have some paté en croûte as well. She hasn't *said* she's pregnant, but she walks around as if she has this great invisible lump in front of her, with an air of radiance, like Christ's mother. Well, she's exactly where he wants her now. He went out shooting rabbits the other day, and tried to get her to make a rabbit pie, but she couldn't bear to clean them. I didn't really like the sound of things. There's always been something about Frank I can't put my finger on ... not quite uncouth, perhaps, but...'

'Uncouth's the word,' said Nick, smoothing his already sleek hair.

'No, it's more a sort of repressed anger, not that he's violent or anything, just, well, a sort of tension. I don't expect we'll see much of them now, because he never seemed to like us, did he? It's a pity, we've been friends for so long. She gave me their change of address card. They've called their place Apple Tree Cottage.'

'How bucolic,' said Nick. 'Shall we have croissants or brioches for breakfast?'

Deborah sat in a deckchair on the lawn, while Peter Rabbit nibbled the grass nearby. She stroked him with her foot. He was warm and soft, and his whole body pulsated as he breathed, like furry little bellows.

'We like it here, don't we, Rabbit?' said Deborah. She stretched her arms above her head, basking in the warmth of the sun. The ears of the corn were dry and brittle, and when the breeze passed through, there was a faint crackling sound. The sun spread its comfortable warmth around her, turning her light brown hair into a halo edged with gold. Deborah began to calculate when she could tell Frank, without a shadow of doubt, that they would have a baby. A few more days, perhaps, just to be sure. She felt part of the natural order of things. The wheat was ripening, growing heavy, the apple trees already showed signs of fruit. She was going to yield to a different scale of time from the 8.33 to Liverpool Street or the 7.30 curtain at the theatre. The time she was involved in was rolling and implacable. Once embarked on, it would rule her life.

In the long grass behind the apple trees, she saw the cat's glinting eyes. It seemed a little less wild, for it did not run away as she got to her feet.

'Come here, pusscat,' she called, crouching on the ground nearer its level. The cat hesitated, as if memories of humans bearing food stirred in its mind. Deborah held out her hand.

'Come on, you want to be friendly, don't you?' The

cat's head withdrew from the grass which half hid it, and it loped away towards the end of the garden.

When Frank arrived home that evening, he said, 'That bloody cat was hanging around by the rabbit hutch. I had to chase it off. You'll have to keep an eye out for it all the time. Throw something at it, shout at it, chase it. You don't want Peter killed, do you?'

During the long afternoon Deborah had wandered in a dream of feeling at one with all living things. Frank pulled her back to the scratchy, everyday life of people getting things done. It no longer seemed the right time to talk about her strange feeling of expectancy inside. She remembered that she had not put the plates into the oven to warm. These things were becoming important to Frank.

His mood improved over dinner and they sat afterwards in the garden watching the sky fade into colourlessness after the sun had set, then darken into night. When it grew chilly they retreated to bed, and left the curtains undrawn to see the night sky.

'There's nothing between us and the stars,' said Deborah, and almost immediately in the stillness there was a shriek, a scream from the garden, like an animal in pain. From the window they saw Peter's hutch in the moonlight, and on top, where the roof joined his wire-netting run, a large black shadow tearing at it.

'Bloody cat!' Frank shouted, and ran downstairs. Deborah put on her dressing gown and followed. In the kitchen, he was feverishly loading his gun.

'What are you doing? The cat's gone. You've already frightened it off,' said Deborah. Frank stared palely and unseeingly at her.

'I've had enough of that fucking animal!' He strode into the garden, the gun under his arm. There was no sign of the cat, but Peter Rabbit was crouched in a corner of his hutch, his eyes protuberant with fear.

[58]

Deborah picked him up and held him close to her until he stopped struggling and lay shivering but quiescent in her arms. They both started at the sound of a gunshot, and Deborah quickly put him back into the hutch and locked the door. Frank was standing by the privet hedge, looking at the ground.

'I've got it,' he said.

The cat lay, limp and bedraggled, on the ground behind the shed. A few hours ago everything had seemed so alive in the enchanted garden, and now here was death, a glinting-eyed creature reduced to an ungainly carcass.

'Why did you do that, Frank? It was so . . .' she felt overwhelmed by words and then finally said, 'so unnecessary. You didn't have any right to do that. It might belong to someone, they might be missing it.'

'Rubbish,' said Frank. 'It was just vermin and it was trying to kill the rabbit. I'll get a spade and bury it.'

The fanatical look had gone from his eyes and he seemed a little shamefaced as Deborah stood over the cat.

'It doesn't look like the one I saw earlier, it's much thinner,' she said. 'It must have been starving.'

'All the more reason to put it out of its misery,' said Frank as he opened the shed door to look for a shovel. A moment later he called, 'There's some mice in here,' and then, 'Oh Christ, Deb . . . come and have a look . . .'

The moonlight slanting through the open door lit up the shadows with cold, bright beams. On the floor was some sacking and in a hollow of the sacking, small, live things stirred and moved. From the clustered heap of fur came squeaks, like a mouse. Deborah saw the tightly-closed eyes, little pale noses, tiny paws furled into bodies, of five newly-born kittens. They were hardly a day old.

She and Frank looked at each other in silence for a moment, then Deborah said, 'She was a mother . . .'

'I wasn't to know that,' said Frank. There was another silence and Deborah was looking at him as if she was seeing him anew. Frank stared ahead of him, his face obstinate and set.

'You can't look after them, if that's what you think. They're too young. I'll have to get rid of them. What else can I do?'

'Do you think that little inlaid table quite fits in with our concept of the flat, so far?' Nick asked Nina as he poured out their after-dinner digestif.

'It's my Biedermeier weapon against your high-tech brutalism,' said Nina. 'There's the phone. I suppose I'll have to answer it. What a stupid time to ring.'

She picked up the phone, and Nick watched and listened with increasing interest. It was from Deborah and she sounded hysterical.

'Oh Deborah, he can't have . . . What, with the gun? . . . How many, *five*? . . . How terrible, and then what . . . Drowned . . . Oh no . . . in a *bucket* . . . Baby, what baby? . . . Deborah, what are you talking about? . . . Yes, you can always come round here, you know that . . . He put them *where*? . . . The *compost* heap? Well, I suppose that's practical, but how awful . . . yes, of *course* they should be buried properly . . . What's this about babies? The cat's? . . . The rabbit's? . . . You're not making much sense, Deborah . . . Yes, I *agree* it's awful . . .' Nina soothed Deborah to the end of the conversation and put the phone down, then turned, with mouth aghast and eyes full of glee, to Nick. As she told the story, he whooped, fell back on the sofa and kicked his heels in the air.

'The lunatic . . . Fearless Frank, the Squire of . . .

Where's the place? Thrappington.' He picked up the change of address card on the mantelpiece, then reached for a biro.

'What are you writing, Nick? Let's see.'

Nina snatched the card from him. Nick had crossed out 'Apple Tree Cottage' and written in wavering letters, like a horror film title, 'Slaughterhouse Five'.

'Oh Nick, you shouldn't, really. Poor Deborah . . .' Then Nina began to laugh. They watched the late night movie, and every now and then they would laugh again, as one or other of them thought of an even better *bon mot*.

It is after midnight, but Deborah is still standing at the open casement window looking out at the garden and the fields. The full moon has turned the landscape into an aquatint of silver and black. Her mind is in turmoil. There will be nights and nights like this, living in isolation with a man I no longer know.

From the bed, Frank says, 'Please come and sleep, Deb.' His hair is ruffled by the pillow and standing on end. The aggression has gone and his face is like an anxious child's. Deborah looks out at the garden. It is quiet and still, not the slightest breeze, and the peaceful land is oblivious to the violence a few hours earlier. The garden has wiped it from its memory, like all the other violence that has happened before. She turns from the window and the moon illuminates her face, which always shows her emotions so clearly. She seems quieter, more subdued.

'Come to bed, Deborah,' says Frank. She takes off her dressing gown and moves away from the shaft of moonlight that brings silver to her hair. For the first time in years, she feels older. That, too, she realises, is part of the natural order of things.

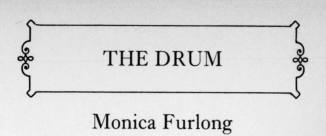

THE DRUM

Monica Furlong

Paul stood on the windowseat and looked down on Miss Brown as she walked out to the waiting cab. The horse, which was big and black, stamped its foot on the frozen road, and the steam of its breath rose into the air. Miss Brown was wearing her felt hat with a bit of grizzled black fur on it which Paul had always thought was made out of her own rough hair. She was carrying her brown leather case. Just looking at her thin back told him that she was angry with him. She opened the door and climbed in without a glance at him, and the cabbie gave an order to the horse, which moved unwillingly off. Paul felt that someone, somewhere, was in pain and that if *She* permitted crying he would have cried. He continued to stand there gazing at the road where the cab had been – now with two steaming brown puddings where the horse had stood, contrasting with the dirty whiteness of the compacted snow. Emily, who was polishing the brass handles with a big yellow duster, spoke to him.

'Like a peppermint?' She produced a tattered paper bag from her pocket. The hot taste on his tongue, or just Emily's kindness, did make him feel a bit better. He turned away from the window to put the peppermint in his mouth and Emily sat down beside him and pulled him on to her lap. He liked the feel of her big floppy body and the warm, stale smell of her clothes; he leaned against her, sucking his peppermint.

'She give you that?' Paul mutely handed her the book in his hand. It had dark blue leather covers with gold writing on the front. They were soft, not like the covers of Papa's books, and inside was thin paper like Mary used under the tiny chocolate cakes; the edges of the pages shone with gold. At the back (he had discovered when he dropped it) were pictures of sheep and men wearing sheets. There was one of a woman about to hammer a big piece of wood through somebody's head which was interesting (he tried to imagine how it would feel to have a piece of wood hammered into your head), and another of a woman with long red hair kneeling on the floor and pouring a jar of honey over a man's feet. He liked the pictures.

'You'll be able to read it when you're a big boy.' Emily's eye fell on the unpolished coal scuttle. She lifted Paul down to the floor.

'She'll be here for lunch', she said. Paul moved away towards the heavy felt cloth that hung over the table when it was not in use; he crawled underneath it and lay full length smelling the dust of the carpet. The gentle gloom of this place, as of somewhere far beneath the sea – the stormy waves clashing too far above his head to trouble him – always soothed him. Even *She* had not forbidden it. It was Emily who eventually summoned him out.

He walked very slowly down the stairs, passing his favourite picture with the boy playing his pipe with his dog beside him, the grazing sheep, the bathing girls with no clothes on, and the man with goat's feet and lovely curly hair. He often imagined going down the path, over the bridge, past the girls (whistling to his dog as he did so), to the meadow beyond. He could roll in the meadow and then find a farmhouse in the blue hills beyond. Possibly *She* would come and look after him. Papa could come sometimes, and smoke his cigar and take him out to eat croissants dipped in coffee at the French bakery.

The sound of his mother's voice brought him back to

the staircase. The drawing-room door was open.

'... worried...' she was saying. Mama's little lapdog, Confucius, was always developing illnesses and troubling Mama. He stood uncertainly in the doorway, looking only at Mama who wore a blue dress which matched her eyes. Her golden hair was in a big bunch behind her head and the colour of it was like one of the fields in the picture where they were cutting the grass with long knives. Mama was pretty but he did not want her in his blue house. As he got nearer to her there was the smell like lots of flowers that he remembered was what he did not like about her. It made it hard to breathe. *She*, on the other hand, smelled of carbolic soap and that stuff they put on you when you cut yourself. Her clothes were all prickly.

'Paul, this is Nannie', Mama said, holding out a hand to him. He took her hand, but did not raise his head. Mama drew him to her and he smelled the suffocating flower smell and felt the slimy touch of silk. He stood with hung head until he buried his face in Mama's side. Confucius, who did not like Paul to touch Mama, snarled.

'There now, you've made Confucius cross', said Mama in a laughing voice, and Paul moved away from her. He could feel the strange person's eyes boring into his back and, not knowing what to do, he hung his head again.

'Why don't you take her upstairs and show her the nursery?'

Paul did not move and after a fraction of a second the new person said, 'Well, I think I can find it. Coming, Paul?' Without waiting to see whether he followed she moved rather lightly across the room and went out of the door and up the stairs. He could feel Mama's surprise and he was surprised himself.

'If you are good you will like her', Mama said, and he

could tell from her voice that the conversation was over. She gave him a little push towards the door, and for want of anything better to do Paul went out and up the stairs. The new person was standing in front of his picture on the landing and examining it carefully. He passed her with blank eyes and went sullenly past her and on up the stairs. She came after him in that light springing way she did everything.

'Race you to the top of the stairs!' she said. He ignored her – *She* had told him never to run upstairs – and continued stolidly on his way. She shot past him laughing, which made him crosser than ever, but then waited for him at the top of the stairs.

'I'm sorry', she said. 'It wasn't fair. I took you by surprise.' He had no idea what she meant, but he could not avoid looking at her, though he quickly looked away again. Her hair was a strange reddish colour, and her skin creamy white beneath it. There were tiny brown spots over the bridge of her nose, and her eyes were brown. He didn't like her.

'Now', she said, 'would you show me which room is mine? I'm longing to see it.' He ignored her and went straight into the sitting-room where the present *She* had given him still lay on the windowseat. Desperately he picked it up; alone with this strange person he had no idea what to do. He could hear her cheerfully opening doors and talking to him and suddenly he saw the tablecloth. He crawled under it again, still clutching his present, and lay on the dusty carpet.

He stayed there for ages until he began to wonder whether the new person had found her room or was wandering disconsolately round the house; he hoped she was. He listened but could hear no sound of any kind. He went out into the corridor; still no sound. He stood outside *Her* room where the new person was to sleep, but could still hear nothing. Finally he turned the handle and pushed the door violently open. The new person had a box on the floor and had taken out clothes and objects and flung them around the room.

'Paul', she said with pleasure. 'Have you come to help?'

He just stood and stared, first at her and her box, then at the room which had changed in a most odd way. There had been some writing in a frame over the bed with forget-me-nots painted round the edge which Paul liked a lot. It said 'Thou God Seest Me' he had been told, and he always had a look round while he was in her room to see if there was an eye hidden somewhere – perhaps in the tiles round the fireplace or the plaster flowers in the ceiling – watching *Her* and him. Perhaps now the eye was watching *Her* in some other room. On the table there had been a big book with little pretty markers in it. He had taken them out and played with them once or twice but she had been very angry with him. There had been a glass by the bed which he had once seen full of teeth which interested him a lot. The glass still stood by the bed but there were no interesting teeth in it now.

'Look, I've brought you a drum', the new person said. She pulled the shining drum out of her box. It was painted on the sides in red and blue and had a red leather string to go round your neck. She pushed it towards him and hunted in the box again for the sticks. When he made no move she seemed puzzled and came across the room to him, lifting the drum and putting the string over his head. She handed a stick to him, but he let it fall to the floor, and he lifted the drum string back over his head, without expression, and lowered the drum to the carpet.

'Oh *Paul*', she said with a maddening laugh in her voice. 'I'll tidy this up later. Let's go and have lunch.' She picked up the drum and sticks and walked out of the room; she put them down on the windowseat beside the book.

After lunch, in the time when *She* used to doze in her chair and had made him sit perfectly still and silent so as not to disturb her, the new person sprang to her feet.

'I'm dying to go out, aren't you?' she said. 'I love this weather. Go and get your things while I get ready.' When she returned in long shiny boots and a coat with a grey swirly skirt and mother-of-pearl buttons, he was still standing there. She went into his room without comment, found his leggings and the buttonhook and lifted him on to the table where she did up the rows of little buttons.

'It's going to be lovely in the Park today', she told him. She eased his arms into his coat, buttoned it up, tucked in his scarf, wriggled his fingers into his gloves, all without help from him. She was not quick and sharp, did not pinch and wrench his fingers, nor appear to be cross at all, but touched him lightly as he might touch a flower he liked. It was odd.

'It's more fun to put on your own things', she remarked, as to some other child who might have been present in the room.

They moved out into the frozen world. The sky was a clear blue and the air so cold that breathing was like eating – you had to think about doing it. He held the new person's hand because *She* had trained him to hold her hand in the street. That other hand had felt quite different, though; it had gripped him in a hard, bony embrace as if it would never let him go. The new person's hand was warm and seemed to have a whole range of expression; when he first took hold of it out-side the house she squeezed it gently, when they got to the Gardens it was so light it was scarcely like holding a hand at all. It made him uneasy.

As on the day before the big boys were sliding on the

Round Pond; yesterday he had wanted to be released so that he might go nearer to them. He would not have dared to go on the Pond itself – *She* had told him how little boys could fall through holes in the ice and freeze to death because they could not scramble out again – but he could have run and jumped along the edge in the hope that the big boys would notice him. Now, as if she read his thoughts, the new person said, 'Wouldn't you like to have a run?' Paul ignored her, and continued primly to hold her hand in silent reproof. Next minute she did something he never forgot. One of the big boys, accidentally or on purpose, had thrown a snowball in their direction, which landed at their feet. The new person let go of his hand, bent down and scooped up a handful of snow. She moulded it quickly with her other hand, then threw it back, laughing; it caught the boy on the shoulder and he laughed too.

'My brother's about his age', she told Paul. For a moment he hoped she might go on about her brother but she walked on with her light springing step, not speaking, but humming to herself.

'Can you whistle?' she asked him after a bit. When she started to whistle a tune he had heard the messenger boys whistle in the street it was really very hard not to push his lips forward to see what sound came out; she had somehow guessed one of his dearest wishes.

'I'll teach you someday soon', she said in a friendly way, just as if he had told her what he felt.

By the time they reached home again Paul realised that he was puzzled by her. She had asked him a number of questions, not insistently, but as things came up, and she seemed not to notice that she never got answers. Had they not told her about him? Perhaps she was stupid, or, more likely, she planned to trick him.

At bathtime he was surprised that the water did not

stop his breath with its cruel, numbing touch, but was warm like a glove. Nor did it hurt when she washed his face and his ears, though he braced himself for pain. As she bathed him she sang in a clear voice that echoed from the tiled walls, not a messenger-boy tune.

'That's an Irish song', she said to him.

When she had finished washing him she pretended the nailbrush was a boat which the enemy wanted to sink with the pumice stone. She splashed a lot and made the walls and floor wet, something Paul had been forbidden to do. He was coldly disapproving. Then when he stood up in the bath she wrapped a big towel round him and took him by surprise by lifting him bodily out, and sitting him on her lap while she dried his toes. She never stopped talking to him and he began to want to be alone in a place where she was not.

Once in bed he lay, as he had been trained to do, with his hands over the sheet.

'Wouldn't you like Rag Doll in beside you?' she asked, and without waiting for a reply she tucked the doll in beside him as if it was real. He thought her very silly. At the same time she picked up the sheet and blanket and tucked his hands down underneath them, smoothing the bed and tucking it in at the sides. It was intolerable. He pulled out his hands, picked up Rag Doll by a leg and dropped her on the floor by the bed.

'Maybe you'll want her later', the new person said without malice. Then she began to tell him a story. He used magic to will her to go away, to leave him to silence and sleep, but in spite of himself it was difficult not to listen to her story about the woodcutter's youngest son and difficult not to laugh when she told him about all the people stuck to the goose in a long line and unable to get away. One day, he thought, he would like to go into the world to seek his fortune.

Finally she stood up, bent over him, and kissed him

[72]

softly on the cheek, ruffling his hair gently as she did so. She turned out the lamp by his bed and went out of the room, but had left a tiny lamp alight on the mantelpiece; he supposed she had forgotten it.

He woke in the night after one of his horrible dreams, but he knew better than to call out. Suddenly, however, he remembered Rag Doll, lying neglected on the floor beside the bed, and he put out a hand and pulled her into bed; seeing the dim little light and burying his face in the doll's stringy hair he could just bear the pain and eventually he went back to sleep.

The next day, and in the days that followed, the book and the drum continued to lie side by side on the windowseat. The new person seemed to feel no need to tidy either of them away, although one day, absent-mindedly, she picked up the drumsticks and played a roll on the drum. It was a splendid sound.

Two days after she came it was Saturday, and as she drew Paul's curtains and came over to sit on his bed – a liberty it seemed to him – she seemed merrier than ever.

'Mama and Papa are going to take you out today', she told him, as if giving him a lovely piece of news and she sprang up and took his best clothes out of the wardrobe. Actually, he did like Saturdays when Papa was home, but he did not see how she could know that. *She* had hated Saturdays and had always been cross when he returned from an outing; that was one of the ways he knew *She* loved him. The new person wanted to get rid of him for a day and he would be glad to get away from her.

Naturally when he returned she denied it.

'I've missed you, Paul', she said. There was a toffee-apple lying on the table. She did not say that she had bought it, and Paul wondered what to do about it. Perhaps Emily had left it for him? He put out a tentative hand and picked it up. He rustled the paper loudly as he undid it, still prepared to renounce it altogether if she laid any claim to having brought it for him as a gift, but she was a reading a newspaper she had bought and did not look up. Paul addressed himself to the hard brown glaze.

After that he began to discover little gifts quite often; he would find a sweet exactly in the middle of his counterpane, crayons and paper on the table in his bedroom, a book with fairy pictures in it lying on the nursery hearthrug. It gave him a lovely warm feeling, but the new person, who was either stupid or cunning, never seemed to notice that he was being showered with gifts. Well, a couple of times she did. One day he came home from a walk and on a chair by the fire there was a mouth-organ. He knew what it was because he had seen a beggar playing one in the street near Kensington Gardens. Trembling with excitement, he picked it up, dazed by the glitter of the sun on its beautiful polished wood surface. He breathed into the holes and a harsh, terrible sound came out; he had breathed too hard. Now he breathed again, softly, and the sound was strong and rich. He tried breathing farther along the mouthpiece and the note was high and piercing. Now almost frantic with delight, he sat down on the floor, and gave himself up without remainder to the mouth-organ. He had no idea how long he had been playing when he looked up and saw the new person watching him. It spoiled his absorption, though she at once returned to reading her book; a sad story she must be reading because she had a tear on her cheek. How stupid she must be not to wonder where the mouth organ came from.

On another day he discovered in his room a clay pipe and a bowl of frothy water. This put him in a dilemma; he had no idea what it was for. He tried drinking the water through the stem of the pipe but it tasted awful. He tried putting the bowl of the pipe in the water and blowing down it; perhaps it was a musical instrument like the mouth organ. It made a gratifying sound but he soon tired of it. There was a secret about this present which he did not know and he could not bear not knowing. There was only one thing for it and he picked up the bowl and pipe and carried it into the new person's bedroom, pushing the door open with his foot. He noticed, vaguely, that it had changed since the last time he was there. A picture of fields and the sea hung over the bed where the forget-me-not writing had been. There was a vase of flowers on the table and photographs – one of the new person herself with her hair down her back standing with some children and grownups. There was a lovely red shawl hanging over a chair. The whole room seemed full of colour and light.

The new person was sitting sewing beside the table and he marched straight to her and put the bowl down beside her.

'What shall I do with it, Paul?' she asked him. He pointed to it.

'What shall I do with it?' she asked him again. Again he pointed and again she looked at him expectantly. After a bit she very slowly picked up the pipe, and put it to her lips. She began to blow and a huge bubble, with curved window shapes white against its soapy blue and rose irridescence, bulged out of the bowl of the pipe, while Paul watched in astonishment. Suddenly it left the pipe and floated across the room; Paul ran after it and tried to catch it but before he could do so it touched the curtain and burst. He wanted to cry out, but by then the new person had blown another one and this time he did cry out because it was so fairylike. His voice came out faint, batlike, not like a voice at all, but the new person did not seem to have heard it. What he knew he must not do is give her the satisfaction of thinking he could make noises; he could imagine her smug pleasure. Yet suddenly he wanted to make noises.

He felt very angry with the new person and he longed for *She* and for the safety of being her good, silent boy who had only to do what he was told for her to be pleased. The new person made everything so difficult and painful. In a sudden longing for *She* he went to the window seat and picked up the book, turning the pages to find his favourite picture of the woman with the jar of honey. There she was, crouching at the foot of the man, her long, beautiful hair falling from her shoulders; she had got the top off the honey, and, in her outrageous way, was starting to tip it over his ankles. As on other occasions, Paul imagined himself as the man, sitting there in his lordly way, letting the woman abase herself. This time, however, it was different. The hair let loose over the woman's shoulders reminded him of the girl in the photograph in the new person's room, and the rich auburn of her hair reminded him of the dazzling pile on the new person's head, and of the wayward strands that escaped and framed her face as she bathed him.

Paul dropped the book and stood up. He was puzzled by a fierce shaking that took his body and worried it like a terrier shaking a rat. Waves of tension seemed to be passing through him, crumpling and stretching his body; somebody was in terrible pain, was so angry that it was not possible to feel such anger and live. He looked desperately about the room for some relief from the ferocity that filled him and his eye fell on the drum. He picked up a drumstick and beat on the drum with all his strength, as he did so uttering a high dreadful cry of hatred and destruction. He was killing the new person, bashing her face in, smashing her head, smattering her limbs, turning her into raspberry jam, and it was wonderful. His voice emerged stronger and stronger as he approached the crescendo of his strength and to his amazement it shaped itself into words. He had often wondered where words came from, how people found them, and everyone but himself had them. Now they hurtled out of him like an express train coming out of a dark tunnel.

'I hate... I hate...' Although he had smashed through the skin of the drum he still kept beating on it, beating on the new person till there was nothing left of the brown eyes that looked at him, the freckled nose, the light hands, the quick step, the twitching mouth, above all of the joyful laugh.

At last he was exhausted. Like someone who has been in another place he came back into his body; his throat hurt with the sounds that had been torn out of it, and he had cut his hand on the drum. Bewildered, he turned round, and there behind him was a young woman looking at him with kindness in her brown eyes. For a few moments they stood and looked at one another, neither making any movement, and then, gracefully, like one who knew what he was doing, he held out his bleeding hand to her and she took it, saying matter-of-factly, 'We must find a bandage.'

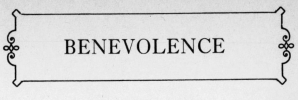

BENEVOLENCE

Jane Gardam

'It's me dad. He's bad.'

The boy on the doorstep was about twelve, and fat. Short-legged and square. 'He's bad.' He pointed into the dark.

He pointed down the Caplan-Fairley's wide suburban drive, so long that it had an ornamental lamppost half-way down it, on a bend, to light the rhododendron bushes, heavy with snow. New snow was beginning to fall on the fat boy and Milo held the door wider to say come in : then, seeing the boy's eyes, instead he said, 'Where?'

Without a coat he ran after the boy down the drive, past the lamp-post and at length to the gates, their four feet making a galloping track in the thick, frosted gravel.

A man lay in the gutter. Despite the rural appearance of the Caplan-Fairley's drive there was a gutter at the end of it and a yellow line, for in the daytime the road was a favourite rush-hour loop-through to the City, ten miles away. Yet now, at night, the house heard scarcely a whisper of traffic.

It was called *Trelawn*, one of a few huge houses standing along a ridge, their gardens sweeping down to the yellow line and spreading amply to either side. The houses were at a greater than geographical distance from each other, garden-wall or parish-pump behaviour being what their owners had moved there to escape. 'You can get away from people here,' they said. 'After London it's wonderful.' At summer-evening parties guests said to each other that they might really

[81]

be in the country. In winter the houses were constantly
burgled.

The Caplan-Fairleys loved *Trelawn* and used it to
the full. From their youth – their very rich youth : they
had always been rich – they had been blessed with a
powerful feeling for those less fortunate than themselves. Their first home had been a Knightsbridge
apartment where they were younger by a generation
than anyone else in the block. Their thick, shocking-
pink carpets and gilt and crystal chandeliers had quite
stunned friends who had known them only as Sociology
students at Birmingham and not quite understood the
reasons for their great self-confidence. College accom-
modation is a great masker of taste.

In the Knightsbridge days the old chums would be
invited for little snacks to show what homely souls the
Caplan-Fairleys really were. 'We pig it,' said Fay, 'We
hardly *use* the dining room,' and served little black-
berry mounds of caviare and frail rolls of Harrods
Parma ham at the marble kitchen table.

Always the Caplan-Fairleys had been dogged, torn
between their feeling of affectionate equality with the
poor and the need to display their own apparently effortless prosperity.

And oh, they were kind. They would lend you anything – their house, their car, their children's nannie –
when they were out of the country and not needing
them. They would lend them even if you were not
needing them either. If you were going to a party Fay
would be round with the best of her heavy jewellery for
you to wear. If you were giving a party Rowland saw to
it that his most expensive pot-plants were delivered for
the evening, though they dwarfed and made listless
your just-arranged garden flowers. When they took you
to Glyndebourne – they took less well-heeled friends
several times a season even though they themselves

were not musical and sat glazed throughout what they called 'the show' – when they took you to Glynde-bourne – it never rained, nobody ever sat in the butter, their hamper was the biggest and best of any on the lawns and their champagne wrapped in the most dazzling napkin. Fay would always ring up a day or two before, to see if she could help you with the appropriate clothes, and afterwards, when you parted from them in the pale dawn, their eyes would meet yours and tell you that they thought absolutely no less of you because you were unused to such perfection. Wonderful hosts, the Caplan-Fairleys. Unenthusiastic guests.

They expected complete loyalty of course. You had to abandon private plans. Everything had to be dropped to take up last-minute theatre seats when some business guest fell out. ('And look, don't feel you have to come on with us to the Savoy afterwards, my dears.') Similarly, if an important business client were to become available after all, you would be expected to give up the seats without demur. There was nobody who could give you a better time than the Caplan-Fairleys so long as you agreed without word to sign to cede all your territory: to accept the image that they had of you, and circulated about you, and never complain or present arguments or ideas of any kind. If you strayed towards an argument or idea the Caplan-Fairleys would look grave. They had no religious interest, no politics, no sense of history. Greece and Italy were a matter of hotels to them. Egypt a great place for racing. The Orient was a poor place for golf-courses and India, of course unvisitable. Yet they were good people, giving much to charity and good works. Much time and much money.

They looked wonderful. Fay wore bright clothes, often white. A good deal of cashmere, hung with gold chains. Her nails seemed always just to have been done, her hair that moment sculpted, her face enamelled like a mask. She was always scented and like an American her clothes seemed always new. She seemed always to have just reached the age that suited her best.

Rowland wore suits of enormous price, perhaps a little tight across the chest, again in a slightly transatlantic way, and also looking eternally new – so new that you imagined they must be off the peg, until you saw the wonderful hand-stitching. And beneath the hand-stitching the chest was strong and broad, bronzed like his face by three good overseas holidays a year. He was relaxed, unhurried, secure – the managing director of his family firm which now was backed by foreign money. He ran his bosses with an overlordly good nature and never slipped up on an employee's name.

But it was their children who were their greatest marvels. There were three. Sons. And not one of them had ever put a foot wrong in his life. The eldest was a barrister, very fashionable but very sound. He ran a Boys' Club in Brixton, boasted black friends yet was a member of the Garrick. The second was in his father's firm and doing splendidly. He was an earnest magistrate and promising skier, tipped for the British team.

The third was Milo, a late joy, born when Fay was over forty, and now nineteen. Milo still lived at home but would be leaving as soon as his final school examinations were achieved. These were proving tardy, but Fay and Rowland knew that it didn't help to worry about one's children's academic achievements just as they knew that they mustn't coddle him for ever.

'We'll throw you out of the nest, won't we Milie darling?'

'Can't wait,' said Milo, eating delicious food cooked for him by the cook from silver polished by the housekeeper and wearing a shirt ironed beautifully by his old nannie.

The man lay in the gutter.

Milo wasn't really spoilt. He was a nice boy. Sweet. Amiable. Nobody knew him very well – perhaps there wasn't much to know. He stayed in his room a lot and had few friends. He did no harm to anyone. The Caplan-Fairleys, experienced in social work with the young, recognised the hazards lying ahead for Milo in their parental excellence. They confided, particularly to their working-class friends, that wealth puts a great burden on a child, especially the youngest. So easy to relax one's standards. To dote. One's ewelamb. Oh dear me, yes.

So, as he grew up, Milo had been sent on various dangerous and taxing pursuits, like rock-climbing or jumping out of aeroplanes, and on the school expedition to Greenland. When he became an experienced climber he had led parties from his brother's Boys' Club, sometimes with other youth leaders, sometimes alone. No friendships resulted from these outings which made Fay a little troubled. She gave parties for Milo, importing many girls. He smiled a lot at the parties and saw to the music. 'He should have slept with someone by now,' said Fay, but Rowland wasn't worried. 'He's a man,' he said, 'He knows how to rough it. For God's sake, that last trip to the Alps they had no doors on the loos. They all slept in their socks.'

The man lay neatly, almost tucked in along the kerb, his face pressed against the grid of a drain. He was narrow. At first he looked not so much a man as a bundle of shabby clothes that might have fallen from some rubbish cart. A bicycle lay near him and another bike, the boy's, lay abandoned across the pavement, one gawky pedal in the air. The man lay still.

'It's me dad. Me *dad*,' the fat boy said again. 'He fell off. He wouldn't get off at the hill.'

Feet came running down the drive and from the house someone switched on the electric flames on the gate-posts. Rowland, his sheepskin coat flapping, stopped between them. 'Don't touch him,' he shouted. 'Ambulance.' But Milo had already flung the fallen bike away and turned the thin bundle over. The gatelights showed a face glossy with sweat, eyes closed, cheek-bones sharp, nose sharper, bared to the snowflakes.

'Kiss of life,' said Milo, and the boy gave a whimper. 'Hold on now,' said his father. 'Steady on.' The man's mouth was purple and slack, hanging open a little. He had terrible teeth. Milo fastened his mouth over the man's mouth and blew into it as he had been taught on his First-Aid class before the Jungfrau. He worked steadily on the man, pressing on him, jerking his arms. Rowland ran back to the house and the telephone and returned with Fay who stood regally, her hair protected by a huge gauzy chiffon, silvery with snow. She pressed the fat boy to the side of her mink-lined rain-coat. He had wet himself. Milo worked and Rowland stood. The boy whimpered again.

'Leave it,' said the ambulance men. 'No go. No good.'

Milo fell back on his heels. Soon the bundle, Rowland and the ambulance-men were gone, the red tail-lights dropping quickly from sight down the hill. After a minute, from where the traffic began, they heard the siren begin to ripple and bleat. Milo, kneeling in the road, bowed his head into the snow and retched. 'Oh God,' said his mother. 'Oh my God – you'll catch some-thing. Go in. Gargle. Wash. Have a bath. I'll get the car.'

'No. I'll come. 'Where d'you live?' he asked the boy,

and put him in the back seat of his car. Fay called a message to someone inside the house, slammed the front door, and got in beside him. 'Me bike!' the boy cried out, as they reached the gates. 'Me Dad's bike. That's a new bike.'

'They'll be all right,' said Fay. 'We've got to tell your mother.'

It was fifteen minutes away, a street of anonymous houses with tight-drawn blinds, and before the car had stopped the boy was out and up the path of one of them and beating against its door. There was no light inside but it opened at once. A voice said 'Is it trouble? Is it police?'

In the hospital Rowland, Fay, Milo, the fat boy and the mother sat in a row and waited. The mother sat still, jaw set, mouth a line. She did not touch the boy who sat apart at the end of the bench. They did not cry. When someone came to say that the man was dead the woman looked startled and began to fumble furtively in her bag for a cigarette and the boy ran out of the hospital into the night.

It took Milo some time to find him and to unhook his hands from the rail fencing off the hospital dustbins. He brought the boy back silently and at length relatives came and stood in a bunch over by the door, hesitant and perplexed, as if trying to remember some old book of rules. At last, uncertainly, they took mother and son away and when Rowland had had a magisterial word with the doctors, the Caplan-Fairleys also went home. Milo stopped off at the gates of *Trelawn* to pick up the bikes. He wheeled them up the drive side by side and without saying goodnight went up to bed and was sick in the bathroom. Fay in the master-suite of the house lay cold in her husband's arms.

After a time Rowland said:

'Heart, poor bugger. Out of work. Second attack. He was thirty-two.'

'Why us? Oh Rowland – why at our door?'

'Where better?' he said.

He lay heavily, imperially, planning what must next be done.

First came the funeral and the cremation. These Rowland organised and the whole Caplan-Fairley family attended. After it he drove the widow and boy home and took away papers and found a solicitor. The next day he spent a long session in the scruffy house trying to discover the widow's income, which seemed to be nil. 'There's the Sup Ben.,' she said, 'That's all. It was 'is heart, see? He couldn't work.'

Then Fay took over, sitting every morning in the airless house as the widow smoked and looked at the fireplace. The widow never questioned any of these visits and seemed neither pleased nor sorry when the Caplan-Fairleys arrived, neither pleased nor sorry when they left. They left her alone – except for their telephone number – for a week.

On the eighth day she rang up and, after a silence, said she wanted to see Milo. She had a present for him. He visited her and was given two magnificent video-recorders.

'Two?' said Milo.

'They're good quality,' said the widow. 'They're both the same.'

'She's given me two videos,' said Milo. 'The best.'

'Oh, there's no real lack of money there,' said Rowland. 'They have everything. I dare say he had a good job before he was ill. They have stereos, microwaves. The boy has a computer. It's their mental security that's damaged. It's the physical shock. They'll come through, but they'll have to be cushioned. It's a great step – giving you these things. They're learning to give.'

'It's funny,' said Milo. 'Two.'

'Most interesting psychologically,' said Fay. 'And rather touching.'

'Or maybe,' said Milo, 'the man was in videos.'

'He wasn't in anything.'

'He might have been in bikes. That's an impressive bike. They're both good. What do we do with them? It'll be upsetting for her if we take them back. I suppose we'd better ask her.'

The widow did not want the bikes back. The boy had quite gone off his and the widow said she couldn't abide the sight of her husband's. They could sell them if they liked. She didn't want to know.

'I'm not sure that we know how to sell bikes,' said Fay, 'but we'll try.'

'Keep them,' said the widow, lighting a new cigarette from a stump; and in the end the barrister son took them for his Boys' Club and found an old sliced loaf and some rancid butter in the saddle-bag of the dead man. He wondered why they had been riding with such things through the night.

'It would be their supper,' said Rowland. 'Poor things.'

'Why were they riding up the ridge anyway?' asked the son. 'Did we ever find out?'

'She said it was for his health. To get exercise. And to get the boy's weight down.'

'We ought to leave them on their own for a bit now,' said Milo unexpectedly.

'So long as they know that we are always here,' said Fay.

The very next day the widow rang to say that she needed help in selling a car. It had to go, she said.

There was no one to drive it. She had to have the money and there was a garage that would take it but no one to take it to the garage.

'Could the garage not come to you?' asked Fay, professionally watching for danger-signals of over-dependence.

'No,' said the widow.

'We'll send down our chauffeur.'

'The mister'd get a better price.'

'I don't think my husband has ever sold a car himself.'

'But it'd look better,' said the widow.

So Milo and Rowland drove down in the Porsche, picked up the dead man's car and proceeded in convoy to the garage. The proprietor looked sharply at them, walked round it, kicked it here and there and gave a glance at the engine. He named a price which Rowland agreed.

'You might as well take this back with you,' said the garage proprietor, lifting a crowbar out of the boot.

'How odd,' said Rowland, 'I've really no use for a crowbar and I'm sure the widow hasn't. I'm sure you could have it.'

'No thanks,' he said, and 'No thanks,' said the widow when it was offered to her.

'We are the owners of a crowbar,' said Rowland to Fay and propped it in the porch. 'A talisman,' he said. 'Videos, bicycles, crowbars. Three triumphs. And she isn't from the present-giving classes. This is a considerable gesture. I wonder why they owned a crowbar?'

A week later the widow telephoned again. She asked to speak to the mister and then fell silent. At last she said, coughing, that the Council would be coming after the house now, and put down the telephone. Rowland, driving to see her found her sitting by the stairs on a broken chair regarding the wall. The boy was in the sitting-room eating Chinese take-away on an upturned box and watching the testcard on the television set. He had not been at school for a week. All the furniture had disappeared. The next day Fay installed them both in the chauffeur's flat over one of *Trelawn*'s garages for they had recently bought the chauffeur his own house half-way up the ridge and nothing could have been more convenient. Widow and son melted into the flat like black-beetles into a wainscot and a new phase of everyone's life began.

At first they seemed bewildered, even frightened. The boy was almost invisible and seen only occasionally slipping round the rhododendrons on his way to the school bus. He and his mother ate Sunday lunch with the Caplan-Fairleys every week – it was a point of principle, said Rowland, and they must attend whoever else was invited. The two sat quietly, looking at their plates, side by side, at the end of the table nearest the kitchen. Other guests sometimes found them rather unnerving, the widow hunched in her chair, smoking between courses, her eyes flickering in what might have been fear or even malevolence. But there she was.

During the week it was her duty to be about the house – to help with cooking, preparing vegetables, and cleaning and Fay would come down to her pretty desk between kitchen and breakfast-room each morning to direct the day, and look her over. Usually the widow seemed just to be sitting, cigarette in yellow hand, cloth and polish neglected before her, eyes fixed on the kitchen television set. A little darkness seemed to go about with her. She was like a smudge in the gleaming rooms. Even the dog went a long way round rather than pass her chair.

'I'd estimate three months,' said Rowland. 'Three months before she is over the shock,' and Fay agreed.

They treated the widow with refreshing brightness, never over-hearty, never cloying. Rowland often put an avuncular hand on her shoulder after setting down in front of her the evening gin and tonic. The widow sat.

'But the boy never speaks at all,' said Fay. 'The mother is silent but the child might be clinically dumb.'

'He's like a rat,' said Milo, who never spoke ill, 'a fat rat. He slopes off to school at daybreak. Leaving the sinking ship. Or as if he's just planted a bomb.'

'But very brave,' said Rowland. 'He passes the place where it happened twice a day, poor lad. He's going to need a lot of care over the next months.'

'He's fairly dreadful. So's his mother when it comes to it.'

Rowland looked gravely at his son.

Yet Milo was fascinated by the pair. He watched them. And he watched them watching him. He felt the boy's knowledge that he was being watched, and his disregard for it. He felt himself mysteriously threatened and found this fascinating, too. 'If you don't mind my saying so,' he said one day to his parents, 'we are being made mugs of.'

But the Caplan-Fairleys did mind, and when the housekeeper and then the nannie began to say the same, they minded more. Rowland gave the widow a bigger cheque for Christmas than he had intended and Fay bought them on impulse some warmer curtains. 'Christmas Day?' said Rowland. 'Of course they'll be here on Christmas Day. Where else can they go? The relations have disappeared.'

'We are making a mistake,' said Milo.

'Duty is never mistaken,' said Rowland. When the widow turned up at the Christmas dinner bearing a brass-gold watch set with diamonds and a strap like a wattle fence – 'Something he got given' – Rowland was delighted and said so. The widow lit another cigarette.

In the New Year Honours Rowland received the
O.B.E: for his long career in good works and public service and it was also his thirtieth wedding anniversary
and the excuse for an enormous party. This was attended by almost everyone he and Fay had ever known,
including for once a scattering of people in positions of
authority. They mixed democratically though somehow not easily among the usual host of the deprived and
the unfortunate. There was a bishop, a judge, a couple
of politicians whose faces you felt you ought to know, a
Liberal peer and a fashionable psychologist. Rowland
was everywhere, moving people about. 'Must split up
the eggheads,' he cried pushing between the bishop and
a Fellow of All Souls with a very bright girl who was his
wife's hairdresser. Sweaty with champagne, he cried to
the psychologist, 'And here's the widow. Our very own
widow. Husband died at our door. Great friends all of
us. Lives with us. Our boy takes her boy rock-
climbing, don't you Milie?'

The widow sat darkly in the middle of the party, chin
in hand. 'Good evening,' said the psychologist without
enthusiasm. The widow scratched her head which had
not been washed for the party. The psychologist felt his
work was following him about. Rowland put an arm
round the widow's unappetising shoulders and
shouted, 'You could take our widow anywhere.' And
Milo hearing these dreadful words saw that the boy
was looking at his father with quintessential loathing.

A moment later, feeling Milo's eyes on him, the boy
turned and looked Milo full in the face and the look of
loathing stayed steady. Fay came forward and began to
heap the widow's plate.

The following day, a Sunday, an icy, foggy day, Milo
was to take the boy rock-climbing in Kent. They had
been together several times before but in better weather

and although the boy was beginning to climb rather well, he was nervous. They were to do a new climb today, rated 'difficult/severe'. The boy had received the news of the outing with his usual, unmoving face.

But as Milo approached the door of the flat over the garage in the early morning he heard a new tune. Mother and son were engaged in raucous and screaming fury. '. . . bloody well staying home,' yelled the boy. '. . . bloody well going and watch yourself or it's all up,' shrieked the widow. Milo stood for a long time on the step before ringing the bell. At length the boy came out.

Two hours later at the top of the climb Milo took in rope for the boy who hung some twenty feet below him, with a hundred feet below that. Milo fastened the rope twice round himself and left all the long length of slack below. Milo then sat down on the cliff-top, and there was silence in the frosty morning.

The boy hung, swinging slightly. 'Hey?' he shouted at last.

Milo sat on.

'Milo?' shouted the boy, 'Hey?'

Silence.

'Milo? Hey. I'm stopped. Milo?'

He began to kick about on the rock, scrabbling his feet. He heaved on his arms and his feet slid beneath him. The rock was slippery. The loose rope had begun to swing.

'Milo! Don't let go.'

At last Milo said – it was so still that he had hardly to raise his voice, hardly to lean forward – 'So, what was the bread for?'

A deeper silence fell upon the cliff and the boy did nothing. In time Milo gave himself a heave and hauled in the rope, and after a time the head and shoulders of the boy appeared at the rock's edge. The two said nothing to each other.

They said nothing to each other for an hour of the journey home and then Milo stopped the car on the hard shoulder, just short of the tunnel into London and looked straight ahead of him and waited.

'You stick it on the glass,' said the boy, 'With butter and that. You don't hear the breaking glass.'

'Did you do it or just your father?'

'He did the break-ins. When I was little, he pushed me in, though.'

'Was he going to push you in a house on our ridge? Into our house?'

'Somewhere. Being fat I wasn't so good as I'd been. He'd been mad at me, getting fat.'

He looked at Milo, 'He'd not know me now. Thinner with the climbing and that.'

'Was your father good? Good at it?'

'What – at thieving? Yes, he was good.'

Milo re-started the car and drove home fast. The boy said, 'He was good all right. That quiet. He was the best, me dad.'

'Did he ever get caught?'

'Oh he'd been caught. He'd done time.'

'Did you mind? Going out with him?'

'No. He was dead good.'

'So you miss it? Your dad, and thieving?'

'I miss thieving. I don't miss me dad. Not now. He'd gone nervous.'

'What's good about thieving?'

'It's exciting. Gives yer a thrill. Gives yer a buzz.'

'Taking people's things?'

'It's not people. It's not against people. It's just it's great.'

'So life's not what it was?'

'It's all right. It's just it's boring.'

'You don't want to change then? Be like – well have

the life I've got?'

'I wouldn't want the life you've got.'

'My parents are good people. Loving people.'

The boy said nothing until they turned in between *Trelawn*'s great imitation torches.

'Why don't you and me go out?' said the boy, 'You'd like it. You'd be dead good.'

'Good day?' called Fay across the parquet. Her face shone with pride at the sight of Milo walking into the hall. So straight, so handsome, so fine and rosy from the bright hard weather. His massive climbing rope coiled over his shoulder was like a knight's shield. 'How did the boy get on?'

'Very well.'

'We'll make something of him. You'll see. *You'll* make something of him, darling Milie. I know you will. Just see.'

'Could you leave it, Ma?'

'Leave it? My darling – '

'Oh leave it, can't you? Can't you grow up?'

Unruffled still, Fay said, 'But you will? You won't drop him? You will go out with him again, won't you?'

'I might,' said Milo. He flung the hard filthy rope across the shining floor, 'I might,' he said. 'You never know.'

DUBE'S FIRST DAY

Ralph Goldswain

Dube lay under the bed, still holding his breath, even though the noise had stopped a long time ago. He didn't know how long, but it was all silent now. He couldn't make himself move and was afraid of what he would see when he did. So he lay there, his eyes screwed tightly shut, every muscle in his body rigid.

Where was Tombi? The last thing she'd said was, 'Under the bed Dube! Quick!' He'd thought she was going to follow him but she hadn't. Nor had she spoken again. Thousands of bullets had come through the window and then there'd been soldiers in the room, but no sign of Tombi. He was afraid to think about it.

And Wilson? He hadn't come home last night. They'd waited and waited and then gone to bed. He had said he was coming.

Dube tried to relax his muscles; to breathe, deeply at first, then more regularly, until he was lying quite calmly, looking up at the bed springs although he couldn't see them in the dark.

He remembered just such an early morning in Soweto when he'd got up to go to the meeting. Wilson Gampu was a prefect at school so when he'd come and asked, Dube had been flattered.

'Come Dube,' he'd said, 'We need you.'

Only those chosen by Wilson were at the meeting and Dube was proud to be there because everybody respected Wilson. Even the teachers were careful when they spoke to him.

'This is nineteen eighty-five,' began Wilson, 'the year of the Cadre. It is a turning point.'

As Dube sat listening, his mind was more on Wilson's clothes than on what he was saying. Wilson always dressed smartly and was wearing a navy blue blazer with its prefect's badge, and clean neat grey trousers. The younger boys hero-worshipped him but Dube was, of course, too old for that. He was sixteen – only two years younger than Wilson. But he admired Wilson and envied his smooth confident manner.

Afterwards, when Wilson asked Dube to join the Umkonto we Sizwe he took his arm and spoke intensely.

'Listen Dube,' he said. 'I know that you are one of us. How would you like to be a freedom fighter?'

Just like that! He was one of the chosen!

'Yes,' he said. 'I want it.' There was something about Wilson that made him want it.

All around him, particularly during the last year, people seemed to be interested only in politics. His mother discouraged political discussions in the house and begged him not to go to any meetings. He had tried to please her but since the riots all gatherings seemed to turn into political meetings.

'You will have to leave school,' said Wilson. His hand was still on Dube's arm.

Dube thought about it. He wasn't doing very well at school anyway. Since they'd burnt the school down last year they'd been having lessons in the beer hall; all the classes crammed together. Their books had been burnt and some of the teachers had left. School seemed a waste of time.

'You will have to leave your mother,' said Wilson.

'But I will see her again?' He looked up at Wilson's serious face.

'In a new South Africa,' said Wilson. 'Only in a new South Africa.'

'My mother . . . began Dube but Wilson interrupted

him.

'She will be proud of you. Like she was proud of your father.'

Dube wasn't so sure about that any more. Now that he was almost grown up she was worried about him. She didn't want him to end up like his father.

'You stay out of politics,' she always said. 'You get your matrick and get a good job. You're a clever boy. You can get your matrick. They need educated boys in Jo'burg. There are good jobs for educated boys.'

'She will be proud of me,' said Dube, looking into Wilson's eyes. Then he looked down again, puzzled, confused. 'But what . . .?'

'You have to fight for your country.'

Wilson spoke sharply, confidently. It was the voice of authority. Dube knew he was right. He knew that was what he had to do. If Wilson said so it was true.

'I will do it,' he said.

'Your father would be happy if he could see you,' said Wilson.

Dube had never known his father – he had died just three months before Dube was born. But he couldn't go anywhere without people telling him stories about the famous Jackson Sela. He was one of the most famous men in South Africa. He'd died in custody and there'd been a big courtcase. His mother had always spoken bitterly about the way the man who'd murdered her husband had turned and grinned at her as they'd left the court.

Dube had been born six days later and the one thing his mother had always said was that she wasn't going to have them take her son as well. So all the day, sitting in the beer hall, instead of listening to the teachers, he thought about how he was going to tell her.

When the time came he spoke plainly. It was just after her favourite programme and she was still laughing.

'I'm going to Botswana,' he said.

She didn't reply. She just threw herself onto the floor and began to wail like a funeral mourner.

'Mama,' he began, and tried to approach her as she lay prostrate on the new carpet she'd saved for two years to buy.

But she just wailed more loudly so he went and sat out in the front, looking at the children playing on the hard red clay street, until the golden clouds turned to an inky blue and the chilly darkness closed in, then he went back. His mother was sitting on the floor, her legs crossed.

'You are your father,' she said, and wouldn't talk about it any more.

It was in nineteen sixty-eight, in the great decade of resistance, that they had taken his father. Then soon after, his family had been visited in the middle of the night and told to collect his body. He had hanged himself in a police cell, they said.

'Never!' his Uncle Harrison had said when Dube had first spoken to him about it a few years ago. 'Your father would never hang himself. They murdered him.'

That was enough for Dube. His mother had always said so too. He had asked Uncle Harrison when a boy at school had taunted him. 'Your father was a coward,' the boy had said, 'He hanged himself.'

But Jackson Sela was a hero and everybody knew about his bravery. Others had been found hanged in their cells in the same month and everybody knew that they hadn't killed themselves either.

The man who'd murdered his father was called de Lange and in his family that was a very bad word. As he grew up the name de Lange came to mean the same as the Devil. In his imagination he used to think of de Lange standing at the courthouse door grinning diabolically, swishing his sharp tail and pointing his horns at him. Then one day he saw a book with pictures of his father's body – a book all about his father and other heroes of the sixties – and there was a picture of de Lange. He remembered being surprised to see that de Lange looked like any other Afrikaner.

His father's reputation brought Dube right into politics in spite of his mother. Phrases like 'your father would be happy,' 'you must do it for your father,' 'your father was a great man,' followed him everywhere he went.

But he was sad about his mother. He wanted to talk to her about it but she knew it would be no good. He knew her well. She was proud of her husband but she was afraid of losing her son too. She had worked hard for the party and that's how she had met Jackson but his death had frightened her. She would never talk politics and he knew that trying to explain to her would do no good. He would just have to go.

So he went.

It was hard to go. Wilson had told him to take nothing and to wear only dark clothes. It was hard to leave his things behind. His mother watched him. Her eyes were dry and all she said was, 'You are your father.' He tried to embrace her but she just stood there making no response.

And then he left. He had to meet Wilson and the others five kilometres out of Soweto on the Krugersdorp road in a big barn piled all round with hay bales. As he walked in the moonlight he wondered why he'd never been out there before. He'd never been in the country. Except the road to Jo'burg. He'd been to Jo'burg about five or six times.

Three other boys were walking along the road too, but Wilson had told him not to talk to anybody, so he looked down and ignored them. They ignored him too

– and each other.

He found the barn, looked for a gap in the hay bales and went in. There were lots of others and he recognised some of them. There were also many he didn't know and he was surprised to see that there were some girls too.

Tombi was there. It had not occurred to him that she could be involved – she was so pretty – and looked as though she would be more interested in being an actress or a model. He had liked her for a long time although he had only spoken to her once.

She smiled when she saw him.

'Dube!' she whispered. 'I knew you were coming.'

'How did you know?' He hadn't even thought she'd noticed him at school.

'Wilson told me.'

It occurred to Dube that she must be a trusted member because Wilson had stressed the need for secrecy.

Wilson was standing in the middle of the barn shining a tiny pocket torch onto a list clipped to the board he was holding, and ticking the names off. There was a strange man with him. Dube couldn't make out his features but he could see that the man was big and bearded. He wore a uniform and his trousers were gathered round at the bottom, beneath puttees. It was almost too exciting for Dube. It was like being in a film.

'I'll see you later,' Tombi whispered and brushed his hand with her fingers. It sent a tingle through him. He watched her go up to the bearded man and touch his shoulder. The man turned to look at her. They were no more than shadows in the moonlight filtering through the gaps in the roof.

Ten minutes had passed since his arrival and it seemed that they were all there now because Wilson suddenly looked up from the clipboard and nodded to the bearded man. Tombi was still standing beside him. Wilson pointed to each one in turn, counting, and Dube counted with him. There were eighteen.

Wilson came towards the door and stood there. All eyes were on him.

'Alright, my brothers and sisters,' he said. 'Follow me. And don't talk.'

He stepped out and they followed him round the side to where, parked in a cave of bales, was a truck. The bearded man got into the driver's seat while Wilson opened the flap at the back. They started to get in. Tombi was beside him again and they sat down together. Wilson closed the flap and they heard the passenger door slam with a tinny sound. The truck started up, vibrating violently, and moved forward, knocking some bales over.

'It is a long journey, my brother,' said Tombi.

'It is Botswana,' he said. 'Only two hundred kilometres.'

She laughed. 'But we are not going directly. We have to go through Bophuthatswana. And not on the main roads.'

He was suddenly annoyed with himself. He felt stupid. Of course they wouldn't be able to go on the big roads.

'If we get caught,' she said, 'they will kill us.'

Dube hadn't thought about getting killed and for the first time he felt the seriousness of it. But he still couldn't think about it.

'Who is that man?' he said.

'That is my father.'

A great relief came over him and he felt like laughing for joy. He couldn't help it and he did laugh.

'Why are you laughing?' she said.

'Because that man is your father.'

She was silent. He was very aware of her presence in

the dark beside him. He wanted to take her hand but didn't dare.

'Is he coming with us?' he said at last.

'Who?'

'Your father.'

'He has come to fetch us. He is an Umkonto captain.'

'What will we do in Botswana?' he said.

'They will take us to Gaberone. Then we'll be sent to army camps for training.'

'The girls too?'

She shrugged. 'I don't know. My father says maybe.'

They were leaving the tarred road now and Dube could smell the dust which came through into the vehicle. They were bouncing and it was uncomfortable.

'When we get to Bophuthatswana they will help us,' Tombi said. 'But it's a long way and you should sleep.'

He didn't feel like sleeping – he was too excited, both by the adventure and by the beautiful girl beside him.

She put her head on his shoulder and closed her eyes. He sat, not daring to move for fear of disturbing her. Her body was relaxed and moved naturally with the truck's bouncing. He remained stiff and his back began to hurt. He wanted to shift his position but sat as still as he could.

The others were talking softly. They spoke of the chance they were getting to stand up to their enemy and to liberate their people. Dube was filled more with feelings about this girl leaning against him than about his country. She was breathing softly and he could smell her hair. He closed his eyes and took a deep breath.

The night dragged on and it seemed that they would never get anywhere. Sometimes they came up off the corrugated dirt roads onto tar. Then it would be like heaven, but it never lasted for long. Most of the time they were either grinding over the corrugations or groaning slowly along rutted tracks. And always the dust.

He hadn't thought it would happen but he fell asleep and woke up in the blue light of morning when the truck stopped. The blessed silence jerked him out of his uneasy sleep. Tombi sat up too.

It was very quiet. The two doors of the cab slammed and they heard Wilson and Tombi's father padding away. Then a dog barked.

'We are there, my sister,' said Dube.

'No, no.' she shook her head. 'Bophuthatswana, I think.'

Then the flap opened and Tombi's father stood there smiling. He leant forward and put his head in. Everybody was awake now.

'We are going over the border soon,' he said. 'But first we will have some breakfast. Come.'

They got up slowly. Dube was stiff, sore and his leg went numb as he stood up. He limped painfully to the back and jumped down onto the yellow earth. Tombi followed, landing gracefully, like a ballet dancer.

They followed her father to a corrugated iron building. The sun was coming up; huge, red, washing the thorn trees with pink. It was very cold.

There was a long trestle table inside the building with thick slices of white bread and jam and mugs of steaming tea. Wilson was spreading jam on the bread.

When they had each taken some food and drink Tombi's father spoke.

'My brothers and sisters,' he said, 'When I look around I see the children of brave parents, children of South Africa, strong and brave. You will not be sorry that you have chosen this path.'

Dube felt proud to be there – to be addressed by this man, Tombi's father.

'We are going into Botswana in a short while,' he continued. 'And once there you will have left your country. But you are only leaving so that you may return in glory to claim for your people that which is theirs.'

The young people cheered. Everybody was happy. Dube looked at Tombi. How proud she must be of her father.

'Now, my brothers and sisters,' he said. 'When we get there we will be going to different houses in the city where you will prepare for your journey into the desert – for it is there – far out of the reach of the Afrikaner – that you are going.'

There were more cheers and the young people put their bread and tea on the floor so that they could clap.

When they had all eaten enough they were taken back to the truck and he helped Tombi up. She left her hand in his for longer than she needed to and he again felt that tingle. Her hand was soft and slightly sweaty.

And then they drove fast for two hours on a straight desert road, then swerved back into the thorny, shrubby veld and finally entered the outskirts of Gaberone with its scattered buildings and dry vacant lots.

Dube and Wilson and Tombi were put in a room with three others. There were six beds in a row, all made up with the same grey blankets. Wilson was now one of them – just another trainee freedom fighter – but Dube knew he would soon be a leader. He knew that Wilson was going to be a great leader.

There were only the six of them in this house. The rest were taken to houses in other parts of the city.

'That's to evade attacks by the Afrikaners,' said Wilson. 'It's very difficult. Gaberone is only fifteen kilometres from the South African border.'

'How long will we stay here?' Dube asked him. They were all exhausted but too excited to sleep.

'Two days,' said Wilson. 'Something like that.'

'So long?'

'There is much to do,' said Wilson. 'This is a proper army. In six months you will be a fully trained guerilla.'

It seemed like a century ago that they were sitting in the beer hall listening to the teacher.

'I wonder what our teachers will think has happened to us,' said Dube.

Tombi laughed. 'They know,' she said. 'What do you think happened to Mr Mkize? He is also an Umkonto officer.'

They finally slept. Dube woke up as the sun was going down. He was cold, and he needed to relieve himself.

In the evening after the meal – dry porridge and oxtail stew – the officers started processing them. They were called in one at a time and the officers filled in forms. Then they went to a doctor where they were examined. The doctor looked at their teeth, their eyes and Dube even had his penis squeezed.

'You are very healthy,' the doctor told him.

While they were waiting their turn they talked. They spoke about the freedom they would bring to their people, about the life they would lead as freedom fighters, and about the future of South Africa as a new African country. Dube knew that he'd done the right thing.

Then they talked about weapons – guns and hand-grenades – and the conversation turned into a babble of excitement as each one shouted his knowledge of weapons. The two girls sat listening. Dube glanced at Tombi. He could see that weapons did not interest her so much. But he couldn't help himself. It was as though this was what he'd been born for.

The next day they were given games to play. They were placed in situations – with problems which they had to solve together. Wilson always took the lead and Tombi usually seemed to find the answers just when they thought they were completely stuck. It was good fun.

In the evening Wilson went off with somebody in a jeep. The others talked a bit – more subdued than on the previous evening – they knew they were leaving for the desert camp the next day – then went to bed. It looked like Wilson wasn't going to return.

Tombi came to him when the others were asleep.

'I am here,' she said simply and slid into bed beside him.

It was as though something he had dreamt about was real. They lay for a long time, close against each other. He kissed her on her cheeks and forehead and felt a deep stirring within himself. They fell asleep in each others' arms.

When the attack came the sky was as bright as day and Afrikaner voices came, metallic, through loud-speakers.

'Stay in your house and you won't get hurt,' they said. 'Do not come out into the street.'

Then there was a noise like the end of the world and Dube knew they were shooting bullets into the room.

'Quickly. Under the bed,' Tombi said, and he rolled down and under the bed and waited for her but she didn't come.

The noise went on for a long time, then stopped. Two Afrikaner soldiers came into the room. He saw their boots, then they left. He heard vehicles starting up and driving off. Then silence.

And now the sharp morning sunlight was in the room. He could see a piece of the wall where that sharpness was blindingly reflected. He edged himself slowly out from under the bed. He couldn't believe what he saw. There was no roof and hardly any walls. The floor and all the beds were piled with rubble. He stood up and looked quickly at his own bed. Tombi lay there, as though asleep, but the blanket which covered her was stiff with dried blood.

He turned blindly away, unable to look at her, and then he remembered Wilson. Thank God he hadn't come home.

He stepped over some bricks and made his way to Wilson's bed on the other side of the room. Thank God, thank God, he kept repeating, mumbling the words with numb lips.

But then he saw that there was somebody on the bed, buried beneath large beams and sections of the roof. He pushed some of it aside to look at the face. It was Wilson. He must have come in after they'd gone to sleep.

Dube looked desperately at the other beds. Everything was twisted and broken – swimming – even more distorted through his tears. But he could see that they were all occupied.

All dead.

There were sounds coming from the street now. Police and soldiers shouted to each other and then Tombi's father was standing in front of him.

'Tombi,' he said and Dube's eyes moved in the direction of the bed.

Tombi's father went over and stood looking at his daughter for a while. Then he turned back to Dube.

'They have attacked all the houses,' he said, 'and others. Innocent people too.'

'How many of us are left?' said Dube.

'You are the third.' He turned back to where his daughter lay silent and unmoving on the narrow bed.

'Are we still going today?' said Dube.

Tombi's father unbowed his head slowly and regarded him. Then he nodded.

'We will go, my brother,' he said.

Dube remembered the deep stirring he had felt when

Tombi lay in his arms and realised, as he looked at the bearded guerilla leader before him, that the stirring was there again, but stronger, different, and growing into something overpowering.

He searched the sad but unwavering eyes of the captain.

'I am ready, Father,' he said.

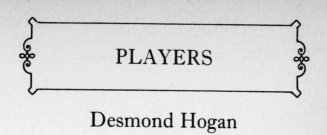

PLAYERS

Desmond Hogan

For the week they were in town each year they changed the quality of life in the town; everybody submitted to them, shopkeepers, bankers, the keepers of the law. There was a light-headedness in puritans and moral flexibility in bigots. They were the players, the people who came to town, performers of the works of Shakespeare ever since the distant, Eamon De Valera mists of the nineteen-thirties. The Mahaffy family gave their name to the players and Ultan Mahaffy commandeered the players. He looked much frailer than before in October 1958 when they came to town; one local woman, a business man's wife in a perennial scarf, referred to him, in passing, in a conversation on the street as looking now 'like a sickly snowdrop'. Ultan Mahaffy should have been happy because 1958 was the first year his only son Cathal had played in the plays since he'd been assigned the roles of little princes, doomed to be decapitated, when he was a child. Cathal had rebelled against the artistic aurora of his family and fled this emanation when he was seventeen to work as a mechanic in a factory in Birmingham. On his return you could see what a strange-looking lad he was: when he had been a child it had been suppressed in him, squashed down, but now he was an albino-like twenty-two-year-old, the whites of his eyes pink roses, the chicken bones of his pale chest often exposed by a loose shirt, his hair shooting up, a frenetic cowslip colour. This mad-looking creature had been given the parts of Laertes in *Hamlet* and Hotspur in *Henry IV part one* in 1958. The prodigal son had returned and conformed to

[115]

the family notion of the inevitability of talent in all its members.

The week before they came the nuns had put on a show in the Town Hall; really a deaf and dumb show, schoolgirls in tights, berets on their heads, rifles by their sides – borrowed from the local army – standing immobile in front of a small cardboard prison that housed a cardinal, (you could see the cardinal's meditative and lowered head through a window, a red bulb behind the cardinal's head). There had been a bunting, made by a nun, of tiny Hammer and Sickle flags above the stage and this, more than anything, had excited gasps from the women in the audience and a round of applause. You weren't sure if it was the cardinal they were applauding for his endurance or the clever idea of the bunting as layers and renewals of applause overlapped. But with the coming of the Mahaffys there was one thing you could be sure of: that the bleeding church behind the Iron Curtain could be forgotten for a week, that this fixation could be briefly abandoned. Only the Lenten missions united people in such common excitement. Immediately prior to the Lenten missions it was the excitement caused by the anticipation of so many sins due to be expunged. Immediately prior to a performance by the Mahaffys it was the excitement of knowing that you were going to be deliciously annihilated for a night by the duress of a play.

Mr and Mrs Mahaffy stayed by tradition in Miss Waldren's Hotel at the top of O Higgins Street. This hotel boasted a back garden inspired by the gardens of the local ascendancy mansion, the garden full, for all its smallness, of walks and willow trees and little ponds drenched by willow trees. This atmosphere was considered appropriate for the heads of the company but all other players stayed as usual with the two Miss Barretts in a more humble bed and breakfast house on

Trophy Street. One of the Barrett sisters was about thirty, the other was near forty, the younger bright, exuberant, bristling with the thought of continual chores to be accomplished, the older usually seated, meditative, lank and arched of cheek. The younger, Una, was small, pudgy, her head powdered with anthracite black and celestial vague hair. The older, Sheona, was, by contrast, tall, demure, red-haired, the fluff of her red hair gripping her ears and her neck like forceps. They'd been parentless for a long time, running a bed and breakfast house since their parents died when Una had just entered her teens. They kept the circus people and the theatre people: many disreputables came to the house, of salesmen only licentious-looking ones, of lorry drivers only those continually drunk. Their family origins had become a mystery for many in town; it was as if they'd had no parents and stepped out of another planet very alien to this town because their manners and their decorum were different. Of the two Sheona was the most faraway. It was as if she'd spent a time in another country and was continually thinking of it as she sat by the natty peat fires that Una had prepared. She was queenly, erect, but was nearing, without the sign of a man, the explosive age of forty.

Much satisfaction was expressed with this year's performances: Cathal Mahaffy, with his mad, upshooting blond hair, was particularly singled out; the redness in the whites of his eyes seemed to be the redness at the bottom of the sky in the evening after they'd gone, the sky over the fair green where the marquee had been. But Cathal hadn't really gone with the show. He came back again and again between performances of the plays elsewhere and it took some weeks before the people of town realised that he was having an affair with Sheona Barrett.

The realisation came in a week of tender weather in November when he was seen again and again bringing Miss Barrett on the back of his motorbike on the backroads between wavering, stone-walled fields in the countryside outside town. The sky was very blue that week, the weather warm, and Miss Barrett, the near forty-year-old, often wore a summer dress, under a cardigan and nothing other than the cardigan for warmth.

How did it happen? What had been going on among the crowd at the guesthouse? More and more women peeped through the curtains and saw the giant tableau on the sitting room wall of Kylemore Abbey, Connemara, the tableau painted onto the wall by a destitute painter from Liverpool once, this work done in lieu of payment of rent. The painter had a red scarf around his neck and women in the town muttered that you'd have to be careful of his piglet fingers, where they went. Now they knew where Cathal Mahaffy's fingers went. They knew only too well. Sheona Barrett had shed forty-year-old skin and become a young woman.

It was Christmas which riled the women most though, Sheona Barrett going up to Dublin to attend a dinner dance with Cathal Mahaffy, at which the lord mayor of Dublin was present. She'd walked to the station, not got a taxi, and some people had caught sight of her on that frosty morning, of the erectness of her bearing and the pink box she carried in one hand. What had been in that pink box? And she still stood straight. People now, mainly women, wanted to knock her off balance. It was fine as long as the theatre came only once a year but now that it had been detained people were disconcerted. Superintendent Scannell, who always dressed in the same withered-looking, yellow ochre civilian coat, was seen chasing his civilian hat along O Higgins Street one morning. A soldier's trousers suddenly fell down as the soldier stood to alert in the square outside the church one Sunday morning. A teacher in the boys' national school suddenly started uttering a pornographic poem in the middle of a mathematics lesson. This man was swiftly taken to the mental hospital. A celibate, he'd obviously been threatened by a nervous breakdown for years. But other people were not so fortunate to get such an easy way out. The theatre had stayed in town and upset people, to the very pegs of their being, those pegs which held their being to the ground just as the players' tent was held to the verdant ground of the fair green by pegs.

Sheona Barrett did not seem even aware that she was upsetting people. That's maybe what upset them the most, that austere bearing of hers. It was a scandal but because it was a scandal that came from the theatre the scandal was questioned. This was the stuff of theatre after all, that people sat comfortably looking at. Now that it had been let loose on the streets you had to ask yourself: was the theatre not an intoxicating thing, like whiskey at a dinner dance? Did it not block out realities? In a way they envied Sheona Barrett for having taken something from a night of Shakespeare in a fair-green and made it part of her life. They all dabbled with the thought of ensnaring some permanence from the theatre and when they realised it was impossible they decided, en masse, to destroy Sheona Barrett's relationship so they could have the theatre back for what it had been, a yearly festive balloon in their lives.

A Texan millionaire had come to live in a mansion outside town in 1957, a mansion in which the caretaker, who'd been there since the rich owners had departed to take up residence in Kensington, London, had murdered his half-wit brother. The millionaire was a divorcee and the parish priest had blocked the entrance to the mansion with his car one morning and stopped the millionaire's tomato-coloured American car from coming out. The priest had got out of his car and approached the millionaire whose head was cautiously inside the car under a wide cowboy hat and informed him that divorcees were not welcome here. The millionaire departed forthwith, leaving his Irish roots.

The same trick was got up to with Miss Barrett but with less success because the parish priest was ill and his stand-in, Father Lysaght, a plump, berry-faced man with his black hair perpetually oiled back, was addicted to sherry, saying mass and giving sermons when drunk on sherry, mouthing out the usual particularities of Catholicism but given new accent by sherry. He was dispatched to pull back Sheona Barrett from her affair, arriving already drunk, was given more drink and spent the night on a sofa with Cathal Mahaffy, discussing the achievements of Cathal's father. Eventually the priest began talking Greek because he thought that was appropriate, quoting poetry about carnal subjects from his seminary days, digging his snout-like nose up into the air as he recited, and then he wavered and snortled his way home. The final agreement had been that only the theatre mattered, nothing else did, and the church and its sacraments palled in comparison to a good theatrical performance. The priest got to the presbytery gates, jolting out a refrain from *The Mikado* remembered from his days at boys' boarding school, boys in merry dress and many in ladies' wigs lined up to daunt the nineteen-thirties with colour and with the smell of grease paint.

The relationship of Cathal Mahaffy and Sheona Barrett had been given a safe passage by the church. Sheona Barrett, by her association with theatre people, had been elevated to the status of an artistic person and as such was immune from the church's laws. You had to titillate people through the arts with a sense of sin so as to reaffirm all the church stood for. A thread united

Sheona Barrett to the artistic establishment of the country now and she knew this, becoming so faraway-looking she looked almost evanescent, as if she was part of the clouds and the fields. Cathal Mahaffy invoked her to many parts of the country and she went swiftly. The townspeople knew now that the girls had been left money they'd never spent much of before. That was evident from the way Sheona Barrett could so readily draw on those funds to get herself around the country. There'd never been any need of that money very much before. Una Barrett groomed her sister, settling her hair. A taxi was often called to speed to some desolate town in the Midlands, past derelict mill houses and past weirs and houses which handed on an emblem for brandy on their fronts, to one another, like a torch.

In August 1959 Sheona Barrett attended the Galway races with Cathal Mahaffy. Her photograph was in the Connaught *Tribune*. She looked like a new bride. In late September they spent a few days together, again in Galway. They sauntered together by the peaceful blue of the sea, holding one another's hands. Most of the holiday-makers had gone and they had Salthill to themselves. The sea was blue it seemed, just for them. The blue rushed at their lovers' figures. There was a happiness for them in Galway that late September. Sheona's hair was a deeper red and often there was red on both her cheeks, 'like two flowerpots,' one bitter woman remarked.

Cathal Mahaffy's body must have been lovely. He was so lithe and pale. In bed with her he must have been like a series of twigs that would seem almost about to break making love to this tall woman. He looked like a boy still. He had this intensity. And he challenged you with his pale appearance, his albino hair, his direct smile. You always ended up for some reason looking to his crotch as his shoulders sloped in his act of looking at you directly.

It was also clear that Cathal's parents approved of the relationship or at least didn't object to it. They were broad-minded people. They were glad to have their son with them and he could have been making love to a male pigmy for all they cared it seemed. They had seen many sexual preferences in their time and a lifetime in theatre qualified them to look beyond the land of sex, to see things that transcended sex; comradeship, love, devotion to art. Art had guided their lives and because of this they themselves transcended the land of Ireland and saw beyond it, to the centuries it sometimes seemed from the look on Mrs Mahaffy's face as she stood on a green in a village, the light from a gap in the tent falling on her face. But there was always tragedy at the end of the route of tolerance in this country.

Shortly before the players arrived in Sheona's town in 1959 Sheona was set upon in a routine walk by the railway station, near a bridge over a weir, and raped. No one could say who raped her but it was known that it had been a gang. She had been physically brutalized apart from being raped and mentally damaged. When she was brought to hospital it was clear that some damage was irrevocable in her. There was a trail of stains like those of tea leaves all across her face when she sat up in bed and her eyes stared ahead, not seeing what she'd seen before. Una Barrett was there, holding a brown scapular she'd taken from its covert place around her neck.

The performances were cancelled that year. There was a mysterious silence around the players. The probable reason was that Cathal Mahaffy had opted out of the main parts in two Jacobean plays that weren't Shakespeare's. He'd made off on that motorbike of his after seeing Sheona in hospital, to mourn. A rape, a job of teaching someone a lesson, had gone wrong. There had been an excess of brutality. The youths who'd run away from Sheona through the thickets by the river had probably been put up to it by nameless and sinister elders in town. That was the hazy verdict handed down. There'd been many accomplices and people, in a Ku Klux Klan way, kept silent about the event, kept their lips sealed as if it had been a figment of someone's imagination and there were often irritated howls years later when the event was referred to.

Sheona Barrett ended up in a home in Galway and she is still there; someone who saw her says her hair is still as red as it was then.

Cathal left the players permanently after the tragedy of October 1959 which months later still spread disbelief. He continued in the theatre in a ragged kind of way for a few years, his most celebrated role being as a black, scintillating cat in one of Dublin's main theatres at Christmas 1960 but after that his appearances became fewer and fewer, until eventually he was down to secondary roles in discontented American plays in the backstreet and basement theatres of Dublin. But his good looks flourished, that appearance of his became seraphim-like, and he was taken up by a rich American woman who'd moved into a top-floor flat in Baggot Street, Dublin and he lived with her as her lover for a few years in this bohemian spell of hers, seen a lot with her in Gajs' Restaurant over its tables regulated by small bunches of red carnations or in narrow pubs packed with Americans and Swedes craning to hear uilleann pipes played by hairy North-side Dubliners in desultory red-check shirts. He nearly always had a black leather jacket on as if he was ready to depart and move on and it was true that no relationship could really last in his life so haunted and fragmented was he by what had happened to Sheona Barrett; he felt irrefutably part of what had happened.

One day he did leave the American woman but she was already thinking of leaving Dublin so there was some confusion about his leaving her; no observer was sure who sundered the relationship.

He spent a few months on people's floor, often on quite expensive antique carpets, around the Baggot Street, Fitzwilliam Square, Pembroke Road area of Dublin. The antique carpets were no coincidence in his life because he was actually working for an antique dealer now who had a shop on Upper Baggot Street and in Dun Laoghaire. The job was kind of a gift, kind of decoration for an aimless person and one Saturday when he wasn't working he did what he'd wanted to do for a long time, drive west on his motorbike to Sheona Barrett's town to try to find what the answer was to a question which had beleaguered his mind for so long: why, why the evil, why the attack, what had been the motivation for this freak outrage, what had been the forces gathered behind it?

But in the town he discovered that there were other explanations for Sheona's state as if she'd been ill all the time. Una Barrett was a housewife, a guesthouse keeper, a mother, the wife of a man who had Guinness spilt all over his already brown jacket and waistcoat. The day was very blue: in the square there was an abundance of geraniums being sold; the sky seemed specially blue for his visit. All was happiness and change here. The past didn't exist. He was an exile, by way of lack of explanations, from the present. But the more he stuck about, wandering among the market produce, the farmers made uncomfortable by the fact he wasn't purchasing anything, the more he knew. People did not like happiness. They distrusted happiness of the flesh more than anything. The coming together of bodies in happiness was an outrage against the sensibilities. It not only should not be allowed to exist but it had to be murdered if it wasn't going to unhinge them further. A swift killing could be covered up, it could be covered up forever; only the haunted imagination would keep it alive and that imagination would, by its nature, be driven out of society, so all could feel safe. There was no home for people like Cathal Mahaffy who knew and remembered.

With money he got from an unannounced source he purchased a house in a remote part of County Donegal in the late nineteen-sixties; the house up on a hill overlooking the swing of a narrow bay. There was much work to be done on it, a skeleton of a grey house peculiar and abandoned among the boulders that all the time seemed about to tumble into the sea. On the back of his motorbike he ferried building materials from Donegal Town. These were the hippie days of the late sixties and blue skies over the bay seemed arranged to greet visitors from Dublin. Often people got a bus to Donegal Town and then there was a liberated jaunt on the back of a motorbike around twists by the sea. There were benevolent fields to one side, the green early Irish monks would talk about, and stone walls dancing around the fields, finicky patterned stone walls. These fields stretching to one side of him like a director's hand Cathal was killed on his motorbike one June day, a Lawrence of Arabia in County Donegal, all his motorbike gear on at the time, helmet, black leather jacket and old-fashioned goggles – a caprice? You felt he was being relieved of some agony he could no longer bear, that the day in June was the last he could have lived anyway, what with the pain in him people had noticed, a pain that scratched out phrases by the half-door of his house, into the Donegal air outside when he was under the influence of fashionable drugs transported from Dublin. One of these last phrases, these last annotations had been – a woman about to play in a nineteen-thirties comedy revival in Dublin had sworn it, her lips already red for the part – 'I don't know why they did it. Why? Why? Why? The innocent. The innocent.' This was mistaken as a premature eulogy for himself and because of it all the young rich degenerates in Dublin who saw themselves as being innocent and maliciously tortured by society gathered by his grave in County Wicklow for the funeral, making it a fashionable Dublin event, a young man later said to have epitomized the event, a young man who wasn't wearing a shirt and was advertising his pale, Pre-Raphaelite chest in the hot weather, a safe distance up from the grave, his chest gleaming, under a swipe of a motorcyclist's red scarf, with sweat and with a hedonist's poise.

Among the crowd from Dublin there were some strange rural mourners but no one identified them and anyway they were jostled and passed over in the crowd so awkward was their appearance, so nondescript was their floral contribution. But someone did, out of some quirky interest, get the name of the town they were going back to out of them. It was Sheona's town and the name was said almost indistinguishably so heavy and untutored was the accent.

Ultan Mahaffy did go back to the town a few times after 1959. The company was smaller but the spirit was still high despite losses of one kind or another. The players were greeted in the town with solicitude rather than with reverence. They were tatty compared to what they had been and the marquee in the fairgreen came to look leprous, unapproachable.

In October 1963 Ultan Mahaffy had a strange experience in the town, one which made him shudder, as if death had sat beside him. A man approached him in Miss Waldren's hotel, a tall man under a yellow ochre hat, in a weedy, voluminous, almost gold coat – the colour of the coat evoked stretches in the middle of bogs, slits of beach in faraway County Mayo; it was a kaleidoscopic bunch of national associations the coat brought but its smell was definitely of decay, of moroseness. 'I beg your pardon, Mr Mahaffy,' a voice said. 'We respect you. You brought art to the town. You'll go down in history. You can't say anything to history. You can't say anything to history.' With that he turned his back and went off. What had he been saying? That Mr Mahaffy could not be impugned because he was part of history. Part of the history books like Patrick Pearse and Cúchulainn. But there had been others who were not quite so fortunate. Mr Mahaffy looked after the man and knew that he would not be coming back to this town.

The following summer, before the new season, Mr Mahaffy had a heart attack in Blackrock Baths in Dublin while walking on the wall which separated the open air pool from the grey Irish Sea. He'd looked an exultant figure in his bathing togs before the heart attack, standing up there, stretching his body for all the children to see.

But anyway Mr Mahaffy's life's work had become irrelevant in Sheona Barrett's town. A few years before, on a New Year's Eve, when snow was falling, screens lit up all over the town with their own snow to mark the first transmission by Irish television.

YOU'RE IN
MY STORY

Philip Oakes

They gave him the room with a view, three miles across Romney Marsh to a Martello Tower, built as a look-out for troops guarding the coast against French invaders. From his window he saw reed beds fringing the Military Canal and tulip fields planted by Dutchmen with money who flew in from Holland in their own light aircraft. It was hardly the place for a Creative Writing course, thought Howard Pine. The setting was more appropriate for historians or writers of cloak-and-dagger stories. For either category inspiration lay all around.

Evening sunlight glimmered on the water-filled ditches and a torn band of cloud darkened to the west. 'We hope you'll be comfortable,' said the Secretary, checking that soap and clean towels had been laid out. 'Give us a shout if you need anything. Drinks in the bar at six. The students will be there to say hello.'

'What are they like?' asked Pine. 'Is there anyone I should watch out for?'

'Watch out for what?' The Secretary's name was Keating. He had a thin red beard which looked like a skin rash and wore bifocals which he was constantly pushing back on to the bridge of his nose.

'Talent,' said Pine. 'Is there any one of them with talent?'

The Secretary shrugged his shoulders. 'There usually is. I'm sure you'll discover him. Or her.' He paused in the open doorway. 'There are three men and nine women on the course. It's the usual ratio.'

'As I recall,' said Pine. 'It should tell us something

about the sexes. Ambitions and so forth.' He turned his
back and did not turn round until he heard the door
close. He was not looking forward to the week ahead,
chiefly because he felt he was there on false pretences.
He did not call himself a creative writer, although he
hoped that now and then he wrote creatively. He wrote
novels which earned their advance and usually showed
a profit for both his publisher and himself. If he was
asked (and occasionally someone put the question) he
described himself as a professional writer. It was his
trade description and he tried to live up to it. Any
writing of merit, he thought, was creative to some
degree, but to isolate that particular strain was embarrassing.

There was also a course on Writing Poetry which was
being given by a middle-aged lady named Margaret
Petrie. Why he thought of her as middle-aged he was
not sure. They were roughly the same age and it was
not a tag that he attached to himself. But studying her
clothes and listening to her reminders about trochee
and spondee, metres which he could never tell apart, he
felt that she had thankfully renounced her youth several
years ago.

They had shared a course the autumn before and
Pine had asked her why she tried to teach what he felt
was an impossible subject. 'It's a challenge,' she said.

'Not good enough.'

'All right. I can't teach them how to write poetry. But
I can teach them the techniques. It's not much, but it
makes the stuff less painful to read.' She poured water
into her whisky and clinked her glass against his. 'Why
do you do it?'

'I've often wondered,' said Pine. 'It can't be the
money because that's a joke. My agent tells me it's
because I need to maintain contact with the young. But
I'm not sure about that.'

'It's the girls,' said Margaret Petrie.

He chewed his lip thoughtfully. 'Do you know,' he said. 'I think you could be right.'

There were always girls on writing courses and one of them usually fell in love with Howard Pine. If she did not fall in love with him she would usually fall into his bed, which, all things considered, was just as convenient and probably less trouble. He was forty-eight years old and since his divorce he had formed no permanent attachment to any woman. Brief encounters suited him very well indeed, although they lacked the emotional excitement which someone falling in love with him provided. He was tall and well-built, with black hair streaked with silver at the temples. Sometimes he was mistaken for an actor who had made British films in the 1960s. He had not put on an ounce of weight in ten years. His teeth were sound. He wore glasses for reading only and he possessed what amounted to a genius for ending affairs which had gone on for too long without causing needless pain to the other party.

He took care to make no promises and never described a future in which anyone other than himself appeared. At carefully adjudged intervals he uttered warnings about his commitment to work and his appalling record as a husband. If someone took him on it was at their own risk. He never gave chase, but frequently he allowed himself to be caught. It was surprising, he sometimes thought, that no one had so far stuck a knife in him. But he was well liked by most people who knew him, even popular, although there were several men who envied him.

What they did not know was that Pine, the successful libertine, the sexual athlete who could still go the distance, was secretly vulnerable. Sex was not all that he required from a woman, nor was it admiration. He was an excellent teacher and he had been of real help to many former students. He had the gift of being able to put himself in their place and, with his added perception, see the opportunities that they would have otherwise missed. He was aware of potential and enraged when it was not put to work. By nature he was an impresario and could not resist giving direction to a life which he felt was drifting out of control. The appeal was irresistible. It was the bait to which he invariably rose and he sensed it whenever it was on offer.

When he walked into the bar that evening he felt it happen once again. A girl stood by the bookcase, a glass of white wine in her hand. Her fair hair was cut short and sleeked back from her face as if she had just emerged from a racing dive. She wore a track suit of dark red towelling and a thin gold chain hung about her neck. Her eyes were pale grey, almost silver. She had a long nose and a wide, tremulous mouth. Several other students stepped forward to greet him, but she held back and Pine did not attempt to draw her into the company.

He watched her as she circled the group, waiting with her arms folded, the rim of the glass pressed against her lower lip. 'Tomorrow morning,' he said, 'I want you to bring an account, not more than five hundred words, of who you are and what you are doing here.' He waved down their exclamations of dismay. 'We have to start somewhere. You're here to work. Let's see what you can do.'

It was a useful stratagem, he had discovered. In the first place it convinced them that he was not playing games. Secondly it curtailed the evening's gossip. After half an hour the really keen ones had already begun to slope off to write their essay.

'Here's someone you've not met,' said the Secretary. Pine looked round with apparent unconcern. 'Hello there,' he said. 'Do you like living on the fringe?'

The girl in the track suit smiled briefly. 'You can see what's going on from there.'

'And join in when it's safe?'

'It didn't look dangerous to me.'

'You never can tell,' said Pine. 'What's your name?'

'Veronica Lowry.' She waited until he offered his hand before extending hers.

'And what do you do?'

'Nothing much. I'm a supply teacher, but I've not been supplying anyone lately.'

'In London?'

'Northampton.'

'And you want to write?'

She nodded. 'I've had one or two things published. Nothing important.'

'But enough to give you the taste for it.' He ordered another glass of white wine. 'What do you want to write?'

'Fiction. Stories. Novels, I suppose. But I'm not sure that I have the stamina.'

'What do you want to write about?'

'Aren't we supposed to concentrate on what we know?'

'It's advisable. At least, it's what I advise. Other people think differently. A lot of them make more money than I do. Mind you, that's easy enough.'

Her hair was so fair it was almost gilt and it was beautiful, he thought, sweeping back in an uninterrupted line, conforming to the shape of her head and pleating like wings in the nape of her neck. Her eyes were almost exactly the same colour and he was reminded of old coins, polished by sand, which had been salvaged from some deep-sea wreck. 'Will you be able to manage your essay?' he asked. 'Do you know what you'll write?'

'I shall write something,' she said. 'The truth, I suppose. I don't know what else I can do.'

It was waiting for him in the common-room when he arrived the next morning. She was sitting in the farthest corner, staring out of the window and she did not look at him as he came in. He read the essays in the order in which he picked them up. Veronica Lowry's was the last, which meant, he supposed, that she had been the first to leave it on the table.

It was much shorter than he had suggested. 'My name', it began, 'is Veronica Lowry. I am 23 years old. When I am in work I teach small children in Northamptonshire. The subjects are commonplace, but my first task is to stir their curiosity so that learning becomes a continuing excitement rather than a duty. They dream at their desks and I wonder how to set their minds alight. With most of them I shall fail and I am saddened by that certain knowledge. They deserve something better and so do I. But I intend to write my way out of the cage. I am here to learn how.'

Pine read the essay a second time and whistled softly through his teeth. The appeal was so urgent, so direct that his impulse was to cross the room to where Veronica Lowry sat in her corner and put his arms around her. He could not do that and he hesitated before continuing with his usual routine of asking students to read their essays aloud for class discussion. The message, he felt, was addressed to him alone. It was not an all-points bulletin.

He shuffled the pages, then stacked them neatly in front of him. 'Thank you for your essays,' he said. 'I'm putting them to one side for the time being, not because they are badly written or inadequately expressed, but because some of them are perhaps more personal than you intended them to be. That's fine. It's the start of good writing. But I want you to think about what you've written for a while longer. Can you take the ideas one stage further before you commit them to paper? Don't lose your first thoughts, but give your second thoughts a chance to emerge.'

It was not bad advice, he told himself, although second thoughts rarely amounted to more than revision. But the emotions that Veronica Lowry had acknowledged were too raw to throw to the class for public debate. He had to protect her until she was less vulnerable.

The day wore on. They discussed style and literary influences, who it was safe to read and who should be read with caution. They analysed a story picked at random from an anthology and talked about writing disciplines and deterrents to writing and, when Pine could no longer avoid it, markets. All writers, he had noticed, whatever their pretensions, wanted to know where they could sell their work and for how much. It was no bad thing, he thought. It helped to define objectives and frequently saved a fearful waste of spirit.

'Whoever you write for,' he said, 'it's important that you describe a real world, inhabited by people with real feelings, saying real things. If you make it real you let your reader into it. They'll trust you and go along with you.' He reached into his pocket and took out a notebook. 'This is the writer's basic tool. You have to constantly look and listen and then write it down. Not just the great thoughts, but the sneaky ones. Think of yourselves as spies, eavesdropping on the universe. What did the woman sitting behind you on the bus say to her neighbour? How does it feel to wake up with toothache? Why is the smell of roasting coffee so marvellous when it hits you in the street?' He waved it in front of them. 'Never be shy with a notebook. Tell it everything and later on it will talk back to you. Tomorrow I want everyone to make a field trip. Keep your ears and your eyes open and get it down on paper. Then we'll think about turning it into a narrative. Okay? See you later in the bar.'

Veronica Lowry did not leave the room with the rest of the class. As he had known she would do, she remained seated, her head bent over her clipboard until he stood in front of her. 'I can show you the way out of your cage,' he said.

She looked up at him. 'I hoped you would.'

'About tomorrow,' said Pine. 'I thought we might make the trip together.'

'Is that allowed?'

'If I say so. There's no reason why not. I have a car. We can drive down the coast.' He held up his hand as though he was testifying. 'I promise you, it's quite in order. What do you say?'

'All right then. Thank you.'

'My pleasure,' said Pine truthfully. 'I look forward to it.'

The next morning they drove through Rye and on towards Camber. It was late October and the caravan camps were deserted. He parked the car in a lay-by, nudging a chain-link fence, and led her through thickets of berberis on to the beach. The bay enclosed them like a giant horseshoe. 'It's five miles across,' said Pine. 'In the summer there's barely room to move. Families, dogs, barbecue parties. I like it better now.'

There had been storms the previous week and the tide-line almost reached the dunes. Small flocks of wading birds probed at the sand and milled around a case of spoiled oranges strewn along the shingle like floats on a fishing net. 'It's a marvellous place for fossils,' said Pine. 'Semi-precious stones too.'

'Such as?'

'Cornelian' he said. 'Amber.'

'That's resin.'

'It still counts.' He took her hand to help her over a

breakwater and held on to it when she was on the far side.

'It's a corny question,' she said. 'But have you been here often?'

'When I was married. My wife was an artist. She used to do landscapes.'

'You mean seascapes.'

'Those too. We were divorced five years ago. Very happily, I might add.' He squeezed her hand and felt no ring. 'You're not married I take it?'

'No one's ever asked me.'

'What if they did?'

'That's not the way out. Why leave one cage for another?'

They drove inland and had lunch in a pub at Pluckley. There was an orchard outside the public bar and they walked through windfalls back to the car. 'This is the most haunted village in England,' Pine told her. 'They say the church has thirteen ghosts, including a dog.'

'Have you ever seen them?'

'Never. Do you believe in ghosts?'

'Ghosts aren't real,' she said. 'I thought we all had to stay tuned to reality.'

It was dusk when they got back. 'Write up your notes while everything's still fresh,' said Pine. 'Come and discuss them later if you like. You know where my room is.'

He let her out of the car at the front door, then drove to the rear of the house to park it. He knew that they had already attracted gossip and he did not care. But there was no sense in adding to it unnecessarily. If they had walked in together she might have been embarrassed and he did not wish to risk that. The next move was up to her.

He went to his room without meeting anyone and

stood by the window. His face was wind-burned and he decided against having a shave. It might appear premeditated, he thought, as if he was planning a seduction. But there was no plan; as always, he was acting instinctively. He had issued an invitation but he had applied no pressure. She was a free agent and whether she accepted it or not was up to her. He knew, though, that she would come, later rather than sooner, probably not until the house was quiet.

The daylight faded and he saw the Martello Tower like a stub of charcoal planted against the sky. When he could see it no longer he drew the curtains and switched on the light. For half an hour he wrote in his notebook, sketching the day's events, detailing what he had seen. He believed implicitly in what he had told the class. He had notebooks going back fifteen years, all carefully filed and indexed. He did not trust his memory; circumstance distorted recollection. But, simply by turning the pages, he knew what he had done and how he had felt a decade ago.

He lay down on the bed and stared at the ceiling. He did not intend to fall asleep, but, much later, he was awakened by the sound of the door being gently closed and without looking he knew that someone was in the room. 'What time is it?' he asked.

'Nearly one,' said Veronica Lowry. 'Is it too late?'

'Too late for what?'

He reached out for her and his hand brushed the back of her thighs. She did not move away and he spanned one leg, rucking the material as he felt for her flesh. She had exchanged the track suit for a dress and his fingers snagged on silk. 'Sorry,' he said.

She did not speak but sat beside him on the bed. In her lap she held a fat blue notebook and Pine took it from her and put it on the bedside table. He moved to one side and she lay down, barely tilting the mattress.

He turned his head and looked into her eyes. She did not even blink but stared back, her expression grave and mildly curious. He pushed the corners of her mouth up into a smile and she allowed it to remain when he took his fingers away. He felt that he was being joined in an experiment by a willing partner; although he was in control, everything that happened was with her consent. He unbuttoned her dress and beneath it she was naked. She had small breasts which lay almost flat against her ribs and her navel was no more than a dimple, as though it had been made with one tuck of the needle.

When he kissed her he tasted fruit and realised that she had been eating oranges. He stretched across her to switch off the light, but she shook her head. 'Leave it on.'

He undressed and as she watched him he was aware of the grey hairs on his chest and the scar which ran from his sternum towards his belly. 'An old operation,' he said. 'I had a duodenal. They severed the vagus nerve. It was the smart thing to do that year. They called it a vagotomy.'

She traced the thin white line with her fingertip and he suddenly wanted an end to the examination. 'Is it all right?' he whispered and she nodded and slid beneath him. It was an easy, practised motion and Pine was at first startled, then reassured. He was not taking advantage of someone who lacked experience. They made love without haste and again he felt that he was under review. He wondered if she had known many other lovers and what comparisons were being made.

When he rolled over to his own side of the bed she did not move, but lay with her forearm bandaging her eyes against the light. He thought of the figure of justice, blindfolded as she considered her verdict. 'Are you all right?' he asked again and she moved her arm and stared at him with her silver eyes.

'I'm fine,' she said. 'That was nice.'

'I thought so too'.

She dried a dew of sweat between her breasts and looked round the room. 'Where's the loo?'

'The bathroom's over there'.

As she crossed the floor he admired her long legs and straight back. The bolt clicked behind her and water sang in the pipes. Pine reached for a cigarette and saw the notebook beneath the lamp. He opened it at the last entry and his own name leaped from the page.

'I walk on the beach with Howard Pine,' said the careful, cursive script. 'The air seems dry, but when I lick my lips they taste of salt as though someone had wiped them with a cloth soaked in brine. The sea makes its own litter. Nylon tow-ropes and bladder-wrack. Chunks of concrete gnawed from a jetty. Plastic bottles. A dead sheep. He holds my hand as I jump over a breakwater and asks me testing questions. It is a necessary game, but the questions themselves are unimportant. We each know how this episode will end. I am in his story and he is in mine.'

It was true thought Pine as he replaced the notebook. He had described the day differently, but in all essentials his account was the same. So were his conclusions. The notebook was where life came together to make a story and, without doubt, one of them would tell it. He could not say who would be first. The bathroom door opened and as she walked towards him he saw the cage dissolve and his role change. The lesson had been learned. They were no longer pupil and teacher. He lifted the blankets and made room for a fellow writer.

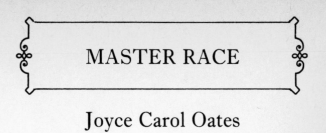

MASTER RACE

Joyce Carol Oates

Why would you want to hurt me?

Why hurt another person?

Though the incident happens abruptly, and the worst of it, in a manner of speaking, is finished within sixty seconds, Cecilia is to remember it in slow motion: the arm pinioning her deftly beneath the chin, the clumsy staggering struggle on the sidewalk, her assailant dragging her into a narrow alleyway, pummelling and punching and tearing angrily at her clothes ... and the rest of it. No warning, no one to blame (she thinks instantly) except herself, for hadn't Philip and the Americans at the Consulate cautioned her against ... She makes an effort, confused and feeble, to protect herself, pulling at the man's arm, using her elbows, squirming, turning from side to side. Stop, please, no, you don't want to do this, *please*, – so Cecilia would say in her reasonable soft-toned voice except for the fact that she can't breathe and her attacker is warning her to keep her mouth shut or he'll rip off her head. Yes the accent is American, low and throaty, South Carolina, perhaps, Georgia – yes, she catches a glimpse of dark skin, long fingers and blunt square-trimmed fingernails, the palm of the hand lighter, almost pale.

Afterwards Cecilia will recall the footsteps hurrying close behind her and her body's shrewd instinct to steel itself against attack, while a more mature – detached – rational – 'intelligent' part of her dismissed the reaction as unnecessary. She is not that sort of woman to succumb to fear, or even to take herself, as a woman, very seriously – not Cecilia Heath.

[145]

Nor is she the sort of woman – she has always supposed – who need fear sexual attack: her vision of herself is hazy and unreliable but she has always assumed that men find her no more attractive than she finds herself.

Now she has been dragged somewhere, her smart linen jacket has been ripped partway off, her skirt lifted – she is being slapped, shaken, cursed, warned – her assailant appears to be both frightened of her and very angry, wildly angry. She doesn't see his face. She doesn't want to see his face. Her body goes limp with terror, she will discover that her clothes are soaked in perspiration, though still, *still*, that amazed stubborn voice of hers, that relentlessly civil voice, is trying to plead, to reason, – *Please*, you don't really want to do this, there must be some mistake –

The man holds her from behind, panting and grunting; awkwardly, and angrily, he jams himself against her buttocks, once, twice, three times; then releases her as if in disgust, thrusts her away, gives her a hard blow to the side of her head; and it's over. Cecilia is sprawled gracelessly on the ground, her nose dripping blood, her breath coming in shudders.

Her assailant is gone as abruptly, and very nearly as invisibly, as he appeared. She hears his footsteps, or feels their vibration, but she can't move to look around. 'Oh but *why* . . . ?' Cecilia whispers. 'Why at this time in my . . . ?'

Fortunately, she thinks, she hasn't been badly injured; perhaps she hasn't been injured at all. Fortunately she is near the Hotel Zur Birke, about three blocks away; and Philip will probably not be waiting for her; and no one has witnessed her humiliation; and no one need know. (Though, surely, humiliation is too extreme a word, too melodramatic? – Cecilia Heath does not consider herself a melodramatic woman. Her

[146]

instinct is simply to withdraw from trouble and attention. In any case she has not been humiliated, she has
been ill-used – the result of bad judgment on her side.)

She gets to her feet shakily, carefully. She dreads
someone approaching, a belated witness to the en-
counter, someone who will discover her in this vulnerable exposed state: an American woman, an American
woman who speaks very little German, not a tourist
precisely, well, yes, perhaps she would be considered a
tourist, with some professional connections, her case
would be reported not only to the Mainz police but to
the U.S. Consulate and to the U.S. Army since her assailant (she knows, she cannot *not* know) was an American serviceman . . . One of the hundreds, or are there
thousands, of American servicemen stationed
nearby . . .

'Oh why did you do it, *why*,' Cecilia says half-
sobbing, 'I meant only to be friendly . . .'

Her right ear is ringing, blood seems to be dripping
down the front of her English silk blouse, she's dazed,
her heart racing, of course she isn't seriously injured;
the assault would not be designated rape; the man
hadn't even torn off her underwear, hadn't troubled.

Nor had he taken her purse, Cecilia seems, relieved.
It is lying where she dropped it, papers and guidebook
spilling out, her wallet safe inside, her passport safe
. . . so there is no need to report the embarrassing incident at all.

At this time – early summer of 1983 – Cecilia Heath
is travelling in Europe with a senior colleague from the
Peekskill Foundation for Independent Research in the
Arts, Sciences, and the Humanities, a specialist in
European history named Philip Schoen. Philip is fifty-
three, almost twenty years older than Cecilia; he claims
to be in love with her though he doesn't (in Cecilia's

opinion) know her very well. He is also married – has
been married, as he says, 'most of his life – not unhap-
pily.' Why does he imagine himself in love with Cecilia
Heath? – she can't quite bring herself to inquire.

In the past fifteen years, since the publication of his
enormous book *The Invention of Chaos: Europe at War
in the Twentieth Century*, Philip Schoen has acquired
a fairly controversial, but generally high, reputation in
his field. Cecilia has been present when fellow historians and academicians have been introduced to
Philip, she has noted their mode of address, a com-
mingling of gravity and caution, deferential courtesy,
some belligerence. She has noted how Philip shakes
their hands – colleagues', strangers' – as if the ceremony
were something to be gotten over with as quickly as
possible. Do men squeeze one another's fingers as they
do ours, Cecilia has often wondered. Do they
dare . . . ?

Though Philip Schoen avidly sought fame of a sort,
as a young scholar, by his own confession 'fame' now
depresses him. Perhaps it is the mere sound of his
name, *Schoen* having taken on qualities of an impersonal nature in recent years, since he was awarded a
Pulitzer Prize, a Rockefeller grant, a position as Distinguished Senior Fellow at the Peekskill Foundation . . . He jokes nervously that his rewards are 'too
much, too soon,' while his wife would have it that they
are 'too little, too late'.

A tall, spare, self-conscious man who carries himself
with an almost military bearing, Philip Schoen is given
to jokes of a brittle nervous sort which Cecilia cannot
always interpret. (Her own humour tends to be warm,
slanted, teasing – not the sort to make people laugh
loudly. She has always remembered her mother and
grandmother murmuring together, in some semi-
public place like the lobby of a theatre, about a fast-

talking young woman close by who was making a small gathering of men laugh uproariously at her wit: *vulgar*, to have that effect upon others.) Philip is impressed by what he calls Cecilia's anachronistic qualities, her sweetness and patience and intelligent good sense; he really fell in love with her (or so he claims – it makes a charming anecdote) when she wrote a formal thank you note after a large dinner party given by the Schoens: the first note of its kind they had ever received in Peekskill, he said. ('Do you mean that nobody else here writes thank you notes?' Cecilia asked, embarrassed. 'Not even the *women* . . . ?') Half-reproachfully Philip told her she was the most defined person of his acquaintance. She made everyone else seem, by contrast, improvised.

Cecilia has only known Philip Schoen since the previous September but she has been a witness, in that brief period of time, to a mysterious alteration in his personality and appearance. His manner is melancholy, edgy, obsessive; his skin exudes an air of clamminess; the whites of his eyes are faintly discoloured, like old ivory, but the irises are dark, damply bright, with a hint of mirthful despair. By degrees he has acquired a subtle ravaged look that rather suites him; his sense of humour has become unexpected, abrasive, inspired. If asked by his colleagues what he is working on at the present time he sometimes says, 'You don't *really* want to know': meaning that doing professional work in the history of Europe, or, by extension, in history of any sort, is a taxing enterprise. Also, he has confided in Cecilia that it's an unsettling predicament to find oneself posthumous while still alive – to know that one's scholarly reputation, like one's personality, is set; that the future can be no more than an arduous and joyless fulfilment of past expectations. Failure is a distinct possibility, of course, but not success: he *is* a success.

'But why call yourself 'posthumous'? – I don't understand,' Cecilia said.

'Perhaps one day you will,' he said.

In late March he dropped by unexpected at Cecilia's rented duplex and asked her rather awkwardly if she would like to accompany him on a three-week trip to Europe. He was being sent by the Foundation to interview prospective Fellows for one of the chairs in history – men in France, Belgium, Sweden, Finland, and Germany; and he had the privilege of bringing along an assistant of sorts, a junior colleague. Was she free? Would she come? Not as an assistant of course but as a colleague? – a friend? 'It would mean so much to me,' he said, his voice faltering.

They looked at each other in mutual dismay. For weeks Philip had been seeking her out, telephoning her, encountering her by accident in town, for weeks he had been watching her with an unmistakable air of suppressed elation, but Cecelia had chosen not to see; after all he was a married man, the father of two college-age children . . . Now he had made himself supremely vulnerable: his damp dark eyes snatched at her in a sort of drowning panic. 'Of course I can't accompany you,' Cecilia heard her soft cool voice explain, but, aloud, she could bring herself to say only: 'Yes, thank you, it's very kind of you to ask, yes I suppose I would like to go . . . but as an assistant after all, if you don't mind.'

He seized her hands in his and kissed her, breathless and trembling as any young suitor. Did it matter that he was nineteen years older than she, that his rank at the Foundation was so much superior to hers, that his breath smelled sweetly of alcohol . . . ? Or that he was married, and might very well break Cecilia's heart . . . ?

On the flight to Frankfurt Philip tells her about his family background in a low, tense, neutral voice, as if he were confessing something shameful.

His paternal grandparents emigrated from the Rhine Valley near Wiesbaden in the early 1900s, settling first in Pennsylvania, and then in northern Wisconsin: they were dairy farmers, prosperous, Lutheran clannish, supremely German. Until approximately the late thirties. Until such time as it was no longer politic in the United States, or even safe, to proclaim the natural superiority of the Homeland and the inevitable inferiority of other nations, races, religions.

'The Germans really are a master race,' Philip says, ' – even when they – or do I mean we? – pretend humility.'

Though he has visited Germany many times for professional purposes he has never, oddly, sought out his distant relatives. Perhaps in fact he has none; that part of Germany suffered terrible devastation in the final year of the war. Yes, he had relatives in the German army, yes, he had an uncle, a much-honoured bomber pilot who flew hundreds of successful missions before being shot down over Cologne.... 'As late as the fifties I had to contend with a good deal of family legend, stealthy German boasting,' Philip says. 'Of course if hard pressed my father and uncles *would* admit that Hitler was a madman, the Reich was doomed, the entire mythopoetics of German-ness was untenable. . . .'

He believes he knows the German soul perfectly, he says, but by way of his scholarly investigations and interviews primarily: not (or so he hopes) by way of blood. Historical record is all that one can finally trust, not intuition, not promptings of the spirit; a people is its actions, not its ideals; we are (to paraphrase William James) what we cause others to experience.

He breaks off suddenly as if the subject has become distasteful. He tells Cecilia, laughing, that there is nothing more disagreeable than a self-loathing German.

'But do you loathe yourself?' Cecilia asks doubtfully. 'And why do you think of yourself as German rather than American . . .?'

Philip takes her hand, strokes the long slender fingers. His gesture is sudden, surreptitious, though no one is seated in the third airliner seat and in any case no one knows them. He says lightly: 'My wife would tell you that the secret of my being is self-loathing – by which she means my German-ness.'

A symposium on contemporary philosophical trends was held that spring at the Peekskill Foundation. No aesthetician participated; no specialists in meta-physics or ethics. There were linguists, logicians, mathematicians, a topologist, a semiotician, and others – all men – who resisted classification. The chairman of the conference began by stating, evidently without irony, that since all viable philosophical positions were represented it was not unreasonable to expect that cer-tain key problems might finally be solved. 'Only in the presence of my colleagues would I confess to such opti-mism,' the gentleman said, drawing forth appreciative laughter.

The sessions Cecilia attended, however, were con-sumed in disjointed attempts to define the 'problems' at hand. Equations were scrawled on the blackboard, linguistic analyses were presented, the philosophers spoke ingeniously, aggressively, sometimes incompre-hensibly, but so far as Cecilia could judge the primary terms were never agreed upon; each speaker wanted to wipe the slate clean and begin again. One particularly belligerent philosopher made the point that the habit of 'bifurcated' thinking, the 'hominine polarity of ego vis-à-vis non-ego,' was responsible for the muddled communication. Which is to say, the custom of thinking in antitheses; the acquired (and civilisation-determined) custom of perceiving the world in terms of opposites; the curse, as he phrased it, of being 'egoed'. Hence civilised man is doomed to make distinctions between himself and others: mind and body: up and down: hot and cold: good and evil: mine/ours and yours/theirs: male and female . . . The list went on for some time, including such problematic opposites as vocalic and consonantal, reticular and homogeneous, violable and inviolable, but Cecilia drifted into a dream thinking of 'male' and 'female' as acquired habits of thinking. *Acquired habits of thinking . . .?*

But why, Cecilia wonders, holding a handkerchief to her bleeding nose, – why hurt another person?

Cecilia and Philip, in Mainz, in Germany, are no longer quite so companionable. In fact they are beginning to have small misunderstandings, not quite disagreements, like any travelling couple, like lovers married or unmarried.

Cecilia speaks very little German, which gives her a kind of schoolgirl innocence, a perpetual tourist's air of surprise and interest and appreciation. Philip's German is fluent and aggressive, as if he half expects to be misunderstood; he responds with annoyance if asked where he is from. Though he had enjoyed himself previously – especially in Paris and Stockholm – he now seems distracted, edgy, quick to be offended. The clerk at the Hotel Zur Birke, for instance, was brusque with him and Cecilia before he realises who they were and who had made their reservations, whereupon he turned apologetic, smiling, fawning, begging their apologies. ('The very essence of the German personality,' Philip muttered to Cecilia, – either at your throat or at your feet.') His eye for local detail seems to be focussed upon the blatantly vulgar – American pop music blaring from a radio in the hotel's breakfast room, 'medieval' souvenirs of stamped tin, graffiti in lurid orange spray-paint on walls, doors, construction fences (much of it in English: KILL, FUCK, NUKE, PRAY) which Philip photographs with a tireless grim pleasure. The enormous tenth-century Romanesque cathedral which Cecilia finds fascinating, if rather damp and oppressive, Philip dismisses as old Teutonic *kitsch*, preserved solely for German and American tourists; the Mainz Hilton he finds a monument to imperialist vulgarity, a happy confluence of German and American ideals of fantasy, efficiency, sheer bulk; even old St Stephen's Church, partly restored after having been bombed, offends him with its stylish Chagall stained-glass windows ... the blue so very pretty, so achingly pretty, like a Disney-heaven.

Cecilia is surprised at his tone, and begins to challenge him. Why say such things when he doesn't really mean them, or when they can't be all he means? – why such hostility? 'I have the caricaturist's eye, I suppose,' Philip admits, ' – of looking for truths where no one else cares to look.'

But Philip is beginning to find fault with Cecilia as well. His objections are ambiguous, likely to be expressed half-seriously, chidingly ... Frankly, he says, she puzzles him when she isn't exacting enough by ordinary American standards; when she's overly tolerant; quick to excuse and forgive. In the hotel's newspaper and tobacco shop, for instance, Cecilia returned a few German coins to the clerk who had, in ringing up her purchase, accidentally under-charged her by about sixty cents; and the man – heavy, bald, bulbous-nosed – became inexplicably angry with Cecilia and spoke harshly to her in German, in front of several other customers. Whatever he said hadn't included the word *Danke*, certainly. 'And you think the incident is amusing?' Philip says irritably. 'How can you take such an attitude?'

'I'm in a foreign country, after all,' Cecilia says. 'I expect things to seem foreign.'

Walking in Mainz on their first evening, trying to relax after the strain of the Frankfurt airport, Cecilia and Philip find themselves in a slightly derelict section of town, across from the railroad station, by the Hammer Hotel, where a number of black American soldiers are milling about in various stages of sobriety. They are touchingly young, Cecilia thinks – nineteen, twenty years old, hardly more than boys. And self-consciously rowdy, defiant, loutish, *black*, as if challenging respectable German pedestrians to take note of them.

One of them, laughing loudly, tries to grab hold of a Binding Bier sign affixed to the hotel's veranda roof, but falls heavily to the street. A driver in a Volkswagen van sounds his horn angrily as he passes and for a minute or two there is a good deal of shouting and fist-waving among the soldiers.

'Strange to see them here,' Cecilia says, staring.

'Yes. Unfortunate too,' Philip says.

They are stationed at a nearby army base, Philip explains, probably employed in guarding one of the U.S. military installations. It might even be a nuclear weapons site, he isn't certain.

Cecilia has been reading about recent anti-war and anti-U.S. demonstrations in Germany, in the *Herald Tribune*. The Green Party is planning an ambitious fall offensive – the hostility to American military is increasing all the time. She feels sorry for these soldiers, she says, so far from home, so young... They must feel

totally confused and demoralized, like soldiers in Vietnam. And so many of them are black.

'Yes. It's unfortunate,' Philip says, urging her along.
'But the situation isn't at all analogous to Vietnam.'

A heavy-set black soldier is staggering about in the
street, clowning for his buddies and two very blond
girls, German teenagers perhaps, who are whistling
and applauding him. Cecilia slows, watching them.
She feels an odd prick of guilt – or is it a confused sort of
compatriotism, complicity? The soldiers are only here,
stationed in West Germany, thousands of miles from
home, because they are in the service of their country;
protecting, in a manner of speaking, private citizens
like Cecilia Heath and Philip Schoen. It is a sobering
reflection to think that, if necessary, the men would die
in that service . . .

When they are some distance away, headed back
toward the Neue Mainzerstr. and a more congenial part
of town, Philip says: 'We're only about one hundred
miles from the East German border, don't forget. It's
easy to forget, in a place like Mainz.'

'What do you mean?'

'I mean that our soldiers are political hostages of a
sort, under the protection of the U.S. Military. Their
presence isn't very agreeable to anyone but it is necessary.'

'"Hostages" . . .?'

'The fact that there are thousands of American
soldiers in West Germany makes it less likely that the
Soviets will attack: it's as simple as that.'

Cecilia draws away slightly to look at her companion.
She cannot determine whether Philip is speaking ironi-
cally, or with a certain measure of passion. Since
coming to Germany he hasn't seemed quite himself . . .
not quite the man she believes she knows. The edge of
antagonism in his voice has the curious effect of provok-

ing her to an uncharacteristic naïveté. 'But is a Soviet invasion a real possibility?' she asks. 'Isn't it all exaggerated as the anti-arms people say?'

'For Christ's sake, Cecilia, nothing is exaggerated *here*,' Philip says. 'Don't you know where you are?'

But still the matter does not rest. Their odd disjointed conversation, their discussion-on-the-edge-of-quarrelling, continues even at dinner. Cecilia supposes it is pointless of her to question Philip Schoen on such issues, her knowledge is haphazard and blurred, much of it, in truth, garnered from the *Herald Tribune* of recent days; but she cannot forget the black soldiers, their foolish conspicuous behaviour, their air of ... wanting to be seen, noted. If Cecilia Heath does not take note of them, who will? Yes, she says, the situation resembles Vietnam in certain ways: an army consisting of many impoverished blacks, very young ill-educated men, men who probably know little about why they are where they are, or even, precisely, where they are. In a way it's a tragic situation.

Philip laughs irritably. He says that, in his opinion, the 'tragedy' is Germany's. He feels sorrier for the Mainz citizens than for the U.S. soldiers. In recent years the soldiers have caused a good deal of trouble in Germany: drunk and disorderly behaviour, drug-dealing to young Germans (even school children), assaults, vandalism, even rape and robbery. Maybe even murder, for all he knew. Such things were hushed up. As for the blacks ... 'The Germans ignore them completely,' Philip says. 'They aren't sentimental about certain things, as we are. They don't assume virtues when they don't have them.'

Seeing her startled expression Philip says that he isn't a racist – she shouldn't think *that* – but he likes to challenge liberal pieties; he wouldn't respect himself as a scholar and an historian otherwise. It is his role as a professional to challenge, for instance, the media's image of such countries as Poland, Czechoslovakia, Hungary. How innocent are they, historically? – objectively? What are their records concerning the treatment of Jews and other minorities, and neighbouring countries? – ('provided the neighbouring countries are weaker'). Fed by a sentimentalist public media, how many Americans know anything at all about Poland's terrifying history of anti-Semitism? – or of Hungary's belligerence against Rumania? – or of the cruelty of the Czechs towards any number of defenceless minorities? One might in fact argue that Poland provoked Germany into the invasion of 1939, for instance, by way of her intransigence in the early 1920s – insisting upon mythical rights against the Germans, and invading German territory by force; invading Lithuania as well, and the Ukraine, and even Russia – in a grotesque attempt to consolidate a little empire. Did anyone in America know? Did anyone want to know? Truth isn't very popular these days.

If the Germans became outlaws, Philip says, who could prove that, following the catastrophic Treaty of Versailles, they were not forced into an outlaw mentality: which is to say – outside, beyond, *beneath* the law? Perhaps Hitler was no more than the Scourge of God.

Cecilia protests faintly, scarcely knowing what to say. Her field of training is art history, particularly nineteenth-century American art; it is probably insulting to Philip for her to attempt to argue with him. Quoting statistics, referring to treaties invasions, acts of parliament, acts of duplicity and vengeance of which Cecilia, frankly, has never heard ('to understand Hitler's Reich, and by extension present-day Germany, you have to understand Bismarck's "siege mentality" of

[158]

the 1880s'), Philip makes Cecilia appear to be something of a fool. What has triggered this episode? Merely the sight of those eight or ten black soldiers by the Hammer Hotel? Cecilia is so upset she drinks several glasses of wine quickly, fighting the impulse to tell Philip that she doesn't care for his facts, his precious History, if they contradict what she wants to believe.

Finally she makes the point that not all Germans are racially prejudiced, as he'd said ('Now Cecilia of course I didn't say *that*') – what of the two young German girls who were with the soldiers by the hotel? They all appeared to be getting on very well together.

Philip shifts uneasily in his seat – they are sitting now in a dim, smoke-hazy cocktail lounge in the Mainzer Hof, as a way of postponing the awkwardness of returning to their own hotel and their separate rooms – and makes an effort to smile at Cecilia, as if to soften his words: 'Those "girls", Cecilia, were obviously prostitutes. No other German women would go anywhere near those men, I assure you.'

It throws you back upon yourself, the starveling little core of yourself – so a friend of Cecilia's once told her, lying in a hospital bed, having been nearly killed in an automobile accident. He meant the suddenness of violence; its eerie physicality; the fact that, as creatures with spiritual pretensions, we do after all inhabit bodies.

It throws you back upon yourself, the starvling little core of yourself. The aloneness.

Cecilia thinks of her assailant, who was not quite visible to her, but irrevocably real. Oh yes real enough – convincing in *his* physicality. She will never know his name, his age, his background; whether he is married; has children; is in fact considered a 'nice guy' when not aroused to sexual rage. (He had been drinking too,

Cecilia recalls the odour of beer, his hot panting breath, the smell of him.) She will never know whether he felt any legitimate pleasure in performing his furtive act upon her, or any remorse afterward. Whether in fact he even remembered what he'd done, afterward. Did men remember such things?

The German prostitutes were so young, no more than seventeen or eighteen, surely. And so blond, so pretty. Cecilia sees them vividly in her mind's eye, she notes their blue jeans, their absurd high heels, their tight-fitting jersey blouses, their unzipped satin jackets – one crimson, the other lemon yellow. She notes their glowing faces, their red mouths, the drunken teetering in the street, the clapping of hands (had the black soldier's antics genuinely amused them, or was their response merely part of the transaction?), the streaming blond hair. *The starveling little core of yourself*, Cecilia thinks. *The aloneness*.

The evidence Cecilia Heath will not provide, either to Philip Schoen or to the authorities: while Philip spent the afternoon at the Johannes Gutenberg University, speaking with graduate students in the American Studies Department, Cecilia, grateful to be alone, spent the time in the Mainz Museum (paintings by Nolde, Otto Dix, Otto Moll which she admired enormously), in the Gutenberg Museum (a sombre, rather penitential sort of shrine, but extremely interesting), and in a noisy pub on the Kaiserstrasse where, believing herself friendly and well-intentioned, she struck up a conversation of sorts with six or seven black soldiers.

It's true that such cheery gregarious behaviour is foreign to Cecilia Heath. She is usually shy with strangers; even with acquaintances; she spends an insomniac night before giving a public lecture, or meeting with her university classes for the first time; someone once advised her – not meaning to be unkind – that she might see a psycho-therapist to help her with her 'phobia'. Yet for some reason, here in Mainz, liberated for a long sunny afternoon from Philip, she must have thought it would be ... charitable, magnanimous ... the sort of thing one of her maiden aunts might do in such circumstances: *How are you, where are you from, how long have you been stationed in Mainz, when will you be going back home, do the peace demonstrations worry you, is it difficult being in Germany or do you find it ... challenging? The German people are basically friendly to Americans, aren't they?*

(Cecilia takes on, not quite consciously, the voice and manner of her Aunt Edie, of St Joachim, Pennsylvania: the woman's air of feckless Christian generosity, her frank smiling solicitude. In the early Fifties this remarkable woman had helped to organize a Planned Parenthood clinic in St Joachim, had endured a good deal of abuse, even threats against her life; but she'd remained faithful to her task. Even after the clinic was burned down she hadn't given up.)

So it happens that Cecilia Heath talks with the soldiers for perhaps fifteen, twenty minutes. Cecilia in her dove-grey linen blazer, her white silk English blouse, her gabardine skirt, her smart Italian sandals. Cecilia carrying a leather bag over her shoulder, a little breathless, shyly aggressive, damp-eyed, her hair wind-blown, a fading red streaked with silver. (She wonders afterwards how old she seemed to them, how odd, how 'attractive'. They were so taken by surprise they hadn't even time to glance at one another, to exchange apprais-ing looks.) She introduces herself, she shakes their hands, she makes her cheery inquiries, she can well im-agine Philip Schoen's disapproval; but of course Philip need not know of the episode.

Harold is the most courteous, calling her Ma'am re-

peatedly, smiling broadly, giving her childlike answers
as if reciting for a school-teacher (he's from New York
City yeh he likes the Army okay yeh he likes Germany
okay there's lots of places worse yeh he's going home for
Christmas furlough yeh ma'am it sure is a long way
off), Bo is the youngest, short and spunky, ebony-
skinned, brash (No ma'am them Germans demonstra-
tin an shootin off their mouths don't worry *him* – how
come she's askin', do they worry *her*). Cash, or 'Kesh',
asked excitedly if she is a newspaper reporter and
would she maybe be taking their pictures...? They
talk at the same time, interrupting one another, showing off for Cecilia and for anyone in the pub who happens to be listening; they make loud comments about
Mainz, about the Germans, about the food, the beer
(they insist upon buying Cecilia a tankard of beer
though it was her intention to treat them to a round);
but two others whose names she hasn't quite caught –
Arnie, Ernie? – Shelton? – regard her with sullen expressions. Their faces are black fists, clenched. Their
lives appear clenched as well, not to be pried open by a
white woman whose only claim to them is that she and
they share American citizenship ... in a manner of
speaking.

Cash half-teases her that she must be a reporter, else
why would she be bothering with *them*, and Cecilia,
flushed, laughingly denies it. 'Do I look like a reporter?' she says. And afterwards wonders why she
made that particular remark.

For an art historian she doesn't always *see* clearly
enough; she isn't exacting; in fact she can be 'perplex-
ingly blind' – so Philip has said, critically, kindly; so
Philip has been saying since their arrival in Germany.
For a critic of some reputation she isn't sufficiently ...
critical. After all, to be sentimental about foreign places

and people simply because they are foreign is a sign of either condescension or ignorance. It can even be (so Philip hinted delicately) a sign of inverted bigotry.

Again and again Cecilia will tell herself that she wasn't condescending to the soldiers, she isn't that sort of person, in fact she feels a confused warm empathy with nearly everyone she meets ... but of course her intentions might be misunderstood. Her empathy itself might be angrily rejected.

Yet is there any reason, any incontrovertible reason, to believe that her invisible assailant was actually one of the men in the pub...? There is no proof, no evidence. The soft gravelly Southern accent might have belonged to any number of Americans stationed in Germany. And of course she didn't see the face. Hearing the running footsteps – feeling the acceleration of her heart – she had not wished to turn her head.

It takes her approximately ten painful minutes – walking stiffly, her arms close against her sides – to get to the Hotel Zur Birke. Only on the busier street people do glance at her, frowning, disapproving, wondering at her dishevelled hair and clothes; but Cecilia looks straight ahead, inviting no one's solicitude.

(Yet it is a nightmare occasion – Cecilia Heath alone and exposed, making her way across a public square, along a public street, being observed, judged, pitied. A dream of childhood and early girlhood, poor Cecilia the object of strangers' stares, in a city she does not know, perhaps even a foreign city: how ironic for it to be coming true when she is an adult woman of thirty-four and her life is so fully her own...)

Fortunately there is an inconspicuous side entrance to the hotel, and a back stairway, so that Cecilia is spared the indignity of the central foyer and the single slow-moving elevator. On the stairway landing she sees her reflection in an ornamental coppery shield: sickly-pale angular face, pinched eyes, linen jacket torn and soiled, signs of a recent nosebleed. The sight unnerves her though it should not be surprising.

She will deal with the situation efficiently enough: she will soak herself in a hot bath, prepare to forget. There is a dinner that evening at eight hosted by a German literary group and Cecilia doesn't intend to miss it.

Her hotel room is on the third floor, near the rear of the building; Philip's is close by. While she is fitting her key in the lock, however, Philip suddenly appears – he must have been waiting for her. He says at once in a frightened astonished voice: 'What has happened to you? Good God – '

Cecilia refuses to face him. She tells him that nothing has happened: she had an accident: she fell down a flight of stairs, five or six steps maybe, nothing serious: nothing for him to be alarmed about.

'But Cecilia, your face, your clothes – is that *blood*? What happened?'

He touches her and she shrinks away, still not looking at him.

Now follows an odd disjointed scene in the corridor outside Cecilia's room, which she is to recall, afterward, only in fragments.

Philip seems to know that something fairly serious has happened to her but he cannot quite think what to do, what to say. He keeps asking her excitedly what *exactly* happened, where did she fall, was it out on the street, were there witnesses, did anyone help her, how badly is she hurt, should he call the downstairs desk and get a doctor, should he call the Consulate and cancel their plans for the evening . . . Cecilia, turned away, half-sobbing, ashamed, insists that she hasn't been injured, it was only a foolish accident, a misstep, a fall, she banged her head and one knee, tore her jacket, her nose started bleeding, she has only herself to blame . . . won't he please believe her?

Philip takes hold of Cecilia's shoulders but she wrenches sharply away, ducking her head. He doesn't repeat the gesture and she thinks, *He's afraid of me*. For some seconds they stand close together, not touching. Each is breathing audibly.

He *should* call a doctor, Philip says hesitantly. She might have a sprain, a concussion . . .

No, Cecilia insists. She *hasn't* been injured, she *isn't* upset, won't he please let her go inside her room?

But he should cancel their plans for the evening, at least, Philip says. He had better call the Consulate . . .

No, says Cecilia, that isn't necessary. If she doesn't feel up to going out by eight o'clock he must go alone, certainly there's no need to cancel this evening, the dinner after all is primarily in his honour and not hers.

But he couldn't do that, he couldn't leave her . . .

Yes, please, oh yes, Cecilia says, trying to calm herself, she isn't at all injured, she's only a little shaken, if she can be alone for a while . . . if she can relax in a hot bath. . . . Please won't he believe her? Won't he leave her alone?

Cecilia has managed to unlock her door. Philip, reprimanded, rebuffed, doesn't try to follow her inside the darkened room. He stands in the doorway, staring, so visibly distraught that Cecilia can't bear to look at him. *He knows*, she thinks. *That's why he's so afraid*.

As Cecilia is about to close the door he says, again, in a faltering voice, that he'll be happy to cancel their plans for the evening if she wants him to. He doesn't want to go to the dinner alone, he'd only be thinking of her, *is* she all right . . . really?

'Yes,' Cecilia says, her face now streaked with tears.

'Yes. Of course. *Yes*. Thank you for asking.'

As she is undressing the telephone rings. It is Philip, agitated, rather more aggressive. Where exactly did she fall? – did someone push her? – was her wallet taken? – why did she stay out so long, alone? – *it was one of those soldiers, wasn't it –*

Cecilia quietly hangs up. The phone doesn't ring again.

In her bath she lies with her head flung back and her eyes shut tight, tight. It is her head that aches, that buzzes, the other parts of her body are numbed and distant. Her buttocks are not sore – they have no sensation at all.

She imagines her mother, her mother's sisters, even her father, her family's neighbours, gathered to sit in judgment on her. Whispering among themselves that Cecilia Heath should not be travelling with a man not her husband ... a man who is another woman's husband ... even if they are not lovers. Especially if they are not lovers.

It isn't like Cecilia. It *isn't* Cecilia.

She recalls her first gynaecological examination at the age of eighteen, the sudden piercing pain, the surprise of it, the uncontrolled hysterical laughter that had turned to sobs ... and hadn't she done something absurd, dislodging one of her feet from the metal spur, kicking out wildly at the doctor? ... angering him so that he'd said something mean and out of character: *You had better grow up, fast.*

And so she did.

But perhaps she did not ...?

In the other room the telephone is ringing. But the sound is faint and distant and not at all threatening.

A long time ago, a decade ago, Cecilia Heath was in

love and more or less engaged, but nothing had come of it; nothing comes of so many things, if you have patience.

She keeps her eyes shut tight so that she needn't see the soldiers' expressions, the grinning flash of teeth, the faint oily sheen of dark, dark skin; she wills herself not to hear again that command, *Shut up, keep your mouth shut*, low and throaty, she had supposed it a Southern accent but in truth it might be any Negro accent at all, New York City, Baltimore, Washington, South Carolina, Georgia, hadn't Bo said he was from Atlanta, and what of Arnie, or Shelton, who had stared at her with such hatred, *Keep your mouth shut or I'll rip off your head*.

She sees no face, no features; she can identify no one; she has nothing to report. Philip is quite mistaken – her wallet wasn't touched. Her passport wasn't touched. Consequently it would be pointless to report the incident to the authorities, pointless and embarrassing to all concerned, the Mainz police, the U.S. Consulate, the U.S. Military Police, pointless and embarrassing, a matter of deep shame to both her and Philip. She has Philip Schoen to think of as well as herself. *Keep your mouth shut or . . .*

She has scrubbed away all evidence of her attacker. Semen, sperm. Perspiration. She has discarded her stained underwear, she will never again wear the linen skirt and jacket, the expensive silk blouse is ruined past recovery, far simpler to fold everything up carefully and throw it away. (She recalls as if from a distance of years her girlish vanity, her excitement, when she bought these clothes for the trip; for her honeymoon fling with Philip Schoen *who claimed to be in love with her*.) No evidence, nothing remains. A few bruises. That ringing in her head, in her right ear. Impossible to press criminal charges against a person whose face you have not seen and whose voice you did not clearly hear, impossible to press charges against such impersonal anger, such sexual rage.

Your feelings are wounded, aren't they. Not your flesh.

You liked the soldiers and wanted to think... yes, badly wanted to think ... they liked you.

*   *   *

Though doomed, the evening begins successfully.

There are nine of them around the table – Cecilia, and Philip, and an information officer from the Consulate named Margot (a German-born American woman, Cecilia's age), and six Germans (five men, one woman) who are writers, and/or are involved in American studies at the University. To disguise her sickly pallor and the discoloration on the right side of her face Cecilia applied pancake make-up hurriedly purchased in the hotel's drugstore – Cecilia, who never wears make-up, who has always thought the practice barbaric – and the result is surprisingly good, judging from the others' responses. (Philip has said very little. Philip is going to say very little to her throughout the evening.)

Yes, the German gentlemen behave gallantly to Cecilia, even rather flirtatiously. Perhaps they sense her new, raw vulnerability – perhaps there is something appealing about her porcelain face, her moist red lips. August who is a philologist and lover of poetry, Hans who teaches English, Heinrich who has translated Melville, Whitman, Emily Dickinson ... and fiery young Rudolph who will shortly publish his first novel ... and even the most distinguished member of the German contingent, the white-haired professor of American history Dr Fritz Eisenach ... all appear to be quite taken with Miss Heath of the Peekskill Foundation. Dr Eisenach addresses her so that all the table can hear, querying her on nineteenth-century American art, in which he claims an interest of many years – for such 'supreme' figures as George Fuller and John La Farge. As it happens Cecilia is the author of a monograph on Fuller, published when she was still in graduate school in New Haven; and her main project at Peekskill is to do a study of La Farge whom she has long considered an important painter ... indeed, it is Cecilia Heath's professional goal to raise La Farge from his respectable obscurity and establish him as a major American artist. So her replies delight Dr Eisenach, and for some heady minutes Cecilia finds herself the centre of attention.

Philip smiles in her direction, sucking at his pipe, saying nothing. When asked about La Farge he professes innocence: he intends to wait, he says, for Cecilia's book.

They talk variously of American art, German art, the journals of nineteenth-century German travellers in North America, the history of Wagner's *Ring* in America, the mingled histories of American and German Transcendentalism in its many permutations and disguises ... they spend a good deal of time on the menu ... the Germans' intention being to treat their guests to a fully German dinner, a representative German dinner, yet not the sort too readily available back in the States. (Cecilia is to sample, with varying degrees of appetite, such delicacies as Räucheraal – smoked eel; Gänseleber-Pastete – goose liver paté: Ochsenschwanzuppe – oxtail soup; Rheinsalm – Rhine salmon; Schweineleber and Schweinhirn – pork liver, pork brains; Hasen – hare; and any number of wines and desserts. The food is hearty and tasty, the Germans speak English fluently, the conversation rarely

[169]

flags. Cecilia feels herself borne along by the very cur-
rent of her hosts' sociability, hearing her own frequent
laughter, glimpsing her reflection in a bay window opposite. (The dinner is being held in a private dining-
room in a restaurant on the Bahnhofplatz, candlelit,
charmingly decorated with oaken beams, paintings of
the Rhine Valley, a massive stone fireplace piled high
with white birch logs. The atmosphere is warm,
gracious, convivial, a little loud. Cecilia wonders how
she and the others appear to passers-by who happen to
glance inside: very like old friends, probably, even relatives, men and women who are extremely close. She
wonders too how Philip and she appear to their hosts.
They are lovers, surely? But lovers who have travelled
together for years, lovers who know each other's
secrets, who have forgiven much, whose courtesy
towards each other has become second nature ...
Called Frau Schoen by the German woman, at the
beginning of the evening, Cecilia felt obliged to correct
her; and wondered if Philip overheard. Frau Schoen,
she might have added, is back home in Peekskill, New
York.)

The talk shifts to politics, the films of the late Fassbinder, an organization in Frankfurt for refugees from
the East, pacific and ecological and vegetarian move-
ments among the young ... Philip and Cecilia will be
flying from Frankfurt to West Berlin on the following
afternoon, they are leaving the Federal Republic of
Germany, consequently tonight's celebration has an
additional symbolic value. Yes, they have enjoyed their
brief stay in Mainz very much. Yes they hope to return
again someday soon. And next time – so August Bürger
insists – they must stay longer, two weeks at least.

Cecilia and Philip glance at each other, smiling, com-
pliant, pretending to be flattered. Cecilia is reminded
of the way Philip and his wife Virginia glanced at each

other from time to time in their home – how effortless it is, to put on a mutual front, to deceive observers. There is even a kind of pleasure in it.

By degrees the dining-room becomes over-warm, the conversation too intense. Cecilia would like to return to her hotel room but cannot bring herself to move. Her head aches again, her breasts are sore. Had her assailant pummelled them? . . . she can't recall. Philip and Professor Eisenach and the shrill-voiced Rudolph are discussing the Green Party, and the international peace movement, and the hoax of the Hitler diary ('a disgraceful episode', the Professor says, shaking his jowls; 'brilliantly hilarious', says young Rudolph), and Aryan mythology, and the manufacture of Nazi memorabilia in the German Democratic Republic, for export to the West. (This too is disgraceful, and cynical, says the Professor; but Rudolph insists that it is justified – if idiots in the F.R.G. want to buy such trash, and kindred idiots in the United States, why not sell it to them? 'Such arrangements are only good business,' Rudolph says.) They discuss the ironies of the new dream of German unity ('a dream acknowledged only in the West', says Hans), and the hunger of all people for national heroes . . . for something truly *transcendent* in which to believe . . . ('So long as the "transcendent" is also good business', Rudolph cannot help quipping, a bad little boy at his elders' table.)

Cecilia drifts off into a dream and finds herself thinking of her mother, but her mother is dead . . . and of her father . . . but, dear God, her father is dead also: they died within eighteen months of each other, during the confused time of Cecilia's 'engagement'. When she rouses herself to attention the atmosphere had quickened considerably. Hans is speaking passionately, his forehead oily with perspiration; August is speaking, laying a hand, hard, on Rudolph's arm, to keep him

from interrupting; Professor Eisenach warns sternly of
the 'Fascistoid' Left; the German woman Frau Lütz
reminds them, should they require reminding, that the
students of the 1920s were far more anti-Semitic than
their teachers and parents – as, she believes, Dr Schoen
himself discussed in his excellent book.

Philip graciously accepts the woman's praise. He surprises his listeners, Cecilia included, by rather con-
temptuously dismissing the peace movement; after all,
he lived through the Sixties in the United States, he'd
been teaching at Harvard at the time, he'd had quite
enough of 'youthful idealism'.

Rudolph begins to speak loudly, excitedly, waving a
forefinger. It isn't clear to Cecilia – part of his speech is
in German – if he is attacking Philip or siding with him.
Perhaps he is attacking the redfaced Eisenach?
Rudolph's sympathy with Socialism, he says, is such
that he has come to the conclusion that the 'forced de-
Nazification' of Germany by the United States was an
act of imperialist aggression; so too, the 'forced demo-
cratization' of Germany. He believes in a Left that is
pitiless and unforgiving of its enemies – especially its
German enemies. He believes in a Left that proudly
embraces German destiny. As for History, he says with
majestic scorn, spittle on his lips and his eyes wickedly
bright, – History has no memory, no existence. If he
had his way he would ban all books written before 1949
. . . which is to say, six years before his own birth.

Philip laughs and regards him with a look of affectionate contempt. 'No German born in 1955 can be
taken seriously,' he says.

Everyone at the table bursts into laughter except
Cecilia and Rudolph, who sit silent.

Belatedly, Margo from the Consulate tries to change
the subject. Did Philip and Cecilia visit St Stephen's
Church, did they see the famous Chagall window? –

but Philip ignores her. He and Rudolph are staring at each other, clearly attracted by each other's insolence. So very German, thinks Cecilia, feeling a wave of faintness. It is an old story that has nothing to do with her.

It is late, nearing midnight. Coffee and brandy are served. Chocolates wrapped in tinfoil. Too many people are smoking, why has no one opened a window...? Frau Lütz who teaches English and American literature at the University asks the Americans their opinion of 'Black Marxist street poetry'; the smiling gat-toothed Heinrich asks about 'revisionist gay' readings of Whitman and Hart Crane. Again the subject of Fassbinder is raised, arousing much controversy; and does Werner Herzog ('the far greater artist', says August) have a following in the States; and is there sympathy for Heinrich Böll, his attitude toward disarmament, his involvement in the blockade of the American military base at Mutlanger...? In the midst of the discussion Rudolph says languidly that he himself would not wish the enemies of Germany destroyed; for as the aphorism has it, our enemy is by tradition our saviour, in preventing us from superficiality. At this August bursts into angry laughter and tells the Americans to pay no attention to Rudolph, who is drunk, knows nothing of what he says, and has never visited the East in any case.

'How dare you speak of my private business! ... you know nothing of my private business!' Rudolph says in a fierce whisper.

It is no longer clear to Cecilia what the men are arguing about, if indeed they are arguing. It seems that Rudolph is only courting Philip, in his brash childish manner ... In the flickering candlelight he looks disconcertingly young; his face is long and lean and feral, his eyes hooded, his lips fleshy. Stylized wings of hair frame his bony forehead, stiff as if lacquered. The

enfant terrible of the Mainz circle, petted, over-
praised, spoiled, he has nonetheless a charming air of
self-mockery. (Unfortunate, Cecilia thinks, that he
isn't qualified to be a Fellow at the Peekskill Foundation – he and Philip would certainly liven things up
there. But it is Dr August Bürger, the philologist-poet
with the impressive credentials, whom Philip has been
interviewing in Mainz.) Now Rudolph and Philip are
speaking animatedly together, for the benefit of the
entire table, of the folly of German submersion in
'European civilization' – that phantasm which had no
existence, could never have had any existence, since
Europe is by nature many Europes, nation-groups,
language- and dialect-groups, clamouring for auton-
omy but, for the most part, fated to be slave states.
Slave states! – does Cecilia hear correctly? Or is she
simply exhausted, depressed? The expression arouses a
good deal of comment on all sides, but Philip and
young Rudolph pay no heed.

Hans, sighing, draws a large white handkerchief out
of his coat pocket and wipes his gleaming face and says
in an aside to Cecilia: 'I am teaching four courses each
term, Fraülein Heath, elementary and intermediate
and advanced English, and am not given to idle specu-
lation, but what of the new Pershing 2 rockets, Fraülein, which your country is so generous as to wish to
store with us? Germany has become a land-mine, Fraülein, in payment for its sins. Do you agree? Are you
informed? The Soviets boast that they will destroy us
how many times, and the Americans are to retaliate by
destroying them how many times . . .? Forty, sixty,
one hundred, five hundred? Yes, Fraülein,' he says,
showing his teeth in a broad damp smile, 'it is only a
joke, no offence is meant, we have here not the privilege
of offence after all. For Rudolph and his comrades the
destruction of Germany is perhaps no loss, as for your

[174]

President Reagan also, just payment for our sins. Please, Fraülein, on the eve of your departure from Mainz, do not take offence – I am but making jokes printed in the newspapers every day, a commonplace.'

Cecilia, flushed, slightly light-headed, would say that she favours peace and disarmament, she doesn't favour war, or even the stockpiling of weapons; but so banal a statement might provoke mocking laughter. Even now Rudolph is laughing with a hearty brutality at something Philip has said, a reference perhaps to the Schoen who flew a bomber for the German Air Force, or is there another Schoen, a Nazi major, about whom Cecilia has yet to hear ... Professor Eisenach makes a passionate drunken speech, his eyes damp and his voice trembling, in Wilhelmian Germany and yet again in the 1930s the Church freely acquiesced to the State, and did the *intelligentsia* protest? Not at all. Never. A disgraceful history of abnegation, a disgraceful history of.... There must be worship, and gods, and devils, and sacrifice; when there are untroubled times it is the peace of apathy and impotence, young men and women indistinguishable from one another in the hair style, costume, behaviour ... it is all *a waiting for the end*. The others listen to the Professor's rambling speech with barely concealed impatience. Then August brings up the subject of the East, addressing the Americans (but Philip especially): Does their country feel sorry for the East Germans? – is their special sympathy for the East Germans? If so they are fools and must be better informed, for the East Germans went from Hitler to Stalin with ease – '*It is all the same to them! The same!*' At this Rudolph stammers in protest; and August accuses him of being a traitor and a fool; and Philip, sucking on his pipe, expelling a thin grey cloud of aromatic smoke, assures the table that he himself feels no sympathy for the East Germans, his sympathy

[175]

is solely for the West Germans, amnesiac for so many years, and made to be on perpetual trial in the world's eyes ... made to feel shame for being German. Indeed, words like 'shame' and 'guilt' strike the ear, Philip says, as distinctly hypocritical. Is German 'shame' indigenous, for instance, or a matter of import? And 'guilt'...?

Several of the Germans propose a toast to Philip, in German, but Professor Eisenach demands to know if Der Schoen is mocking them? What can such sympathy mean?

'But Professor, we are foolish to question sympathy, from any quarter!' Frau Lütz says chidingly.

'You carried it off quite well,' Philip tells Cecilia quietly on their way back to the Hotel Zur Birke. His voice is just perceptibly slurred; there is a slight drag to his heels. But clearly he is in high spirits – a good deal of his soul has been restored.

Cecilia doesn't ask what he means. She says, 'And so did you.'

But Philip, keyed up, nervous, isn't ready to end the day, the long festive celebratory evening. He finds his hotel room depressing, as he has said several times, would Cecilia care to have a final drink, a nightcap, at that Rathskeller up the street...? Philip is pale, smiling, ageing around the eyes, a wifeless husband, a lover without a beloved, clearly deserving of female sympathy. But Cecilia is suffused with a sense of irony as if her very flesh might laugh; Cecilia draws unobtrusively away. They have not touched since that awkward meeting in the hotel corridor – they have hardly dared look at each other all evening. Cecilia understands that it falls to her to assuage this man's guilt for thinking her despoiled by denying the very premise for such thinking, she understands that he is eager as a small child to be assuaged, eager to believe whatever she tells him; but she does not intend to tell him anything.

They are standing in front of the Hotel Zur Birke, a solitary tourist couple, apparently indecisive about what to do next. It is late, past midnight, the wind has picked up, clearly Mainz is not Frankfurt or Berlin in terms of its night-life, why not give up, why not simply go to bed? But Philip doesn't want to go to bed alone. Philip seems to be frightened of being alone. He detains Cecilia, asking what she thought of the Germans at dinner. Wasn't it all supremely revealing? The casual remarks as well as the political – ? That quintessential Germanness he'd find amusing if it weren't so terrifying – the secret gloating pride in their blood, in their race – in sin, guilt, history, whatever they choose to call it –

Cecilia surprises him by laughing, laughing almost heartily, as she slips past him and enters the hotel.

There, in her room on the third floor, she falls asleep almost at once, as soon as she turns out the light and finds a comfortable position in her bed. She will not be accompanying Philip to West Berlin the next day – she will make her own arrangements at the Frankfurt airport to fly back home. It should not be very difficult, she thinks; even informing Philip about her decision should not be very difficult. She supposes he will understand.

He will never have to touch me again, she thinks.

Released, profoundly relieved, she sinks through diaphanous layers of sleep, aware of herself sinking, drifting downward, her physical weight dissolved. She sees a creek out of her childhood – the St Joachim – she smells the wet, newly-mowed grass in the cemetery where both her parents are buried – she hears her Aunt

Edie's voice raised in welcome: Cecilia, a child of eight or nine, shyly poking her head into her aunt's kitchen, standing on the rear porch, holding the screen door open. It is summer but quite windy. Raindrops the size of golf balls are pelting the roof. A river has overflowed its banks, a lake has overflowed, the very light is strange pale and glowering, a sunken city is rising slowly to the surface, a city of spires, towers, old battlements, partly in ruins, blackened by fire ... and now a cathedral of massive dimensions, its highest tower partly crumbled, its edifice stark and grim ... and now a cobblestone street, puddled with bright water that strikes the eye like flame ... Cecilia, alone, is half-running along the empty street, she is both relieved that it is empty and on the brink of terror, for what if she is lost? – yet she cannot be lost since she seems to know where she is headed, hurrying forward as if in full possession of her senses, looking neither to the left nor the right. She is barefoot, only partly dressed. She is breathless with fear. No matter, she seems to know where she is going, behind her footsteps suddenly sound, close behind her, overtaking her, but she does not intend to turn her head.

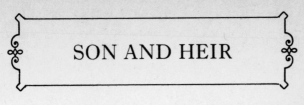

SON AND HEIR

Piers Paul Read

The birth of little Henry Carter-Clark, which was announced in the *Times* in the way births of Carter-Clarks had been announced in the *Times* for many generations, was, like the computer typesetting of the announcement itself, a blend of old-fashioned custom and modern technology.

Amelia Carter-Clark had, as everyone knew, been trying for some time to have a boy. She had had first one, then a second, then third little girl – the first and third as pretty as their mother, the second 'full of character'. At each delivery both Amelia and Adam, her husband, had been obliged to make a little more effort to conceal their disappointment that she had not given birth to a son and heir.

It is common in certain classes and cultures to want a son. Among the ancient Greeks and the primitive Chinese girls were sometimes smothered at birth. Adam Carter-Clark, of course, was neither an ancient Greek nor a primitive Chinese but came from that rare, but not extinct, breed of English landed gentlemen. He was Sir Adam Carter-Clark, Bt., and owned a two thousand acre estate in Wiltshire called Parkham Court. Parkham was subject to entail – a quaint old law, as old as the Carter-Clark family, which meant that the house and land, like the title, could only be inherited by a male heir.

There was no danger that the name of Carter-Clark, made illustrious by Admiral Sir George Carter-Clark in the Napoleonic wars, would become extinct because Adam Carter-Clark had besides his six older sisters a younger brother, Martin, who was married and had three sons. His wife, Jennifer, who had worked as in the research department of the stockbroking firm in which Martin was a partner, was not only intelligent but remarkably fertile: there were two daughters as well as the three sons. Nothing was ever said, of course, because the English never bring things out into the open, but as the years went by, and Amelia only gave birth to daughters, Martin and Jennifer Carter-Clark took on a slightly smug look whenever they came *en famille* to stay at Parkham Court. They even took to strolling around the magnificent eighteenth-century house with an almost proprietorial air. Worst of all old Nanny Liddle, who had looked after both Adam and Martin as children and was now employed by Adam to look after his three little girls, had taken to smiling in a particular way at Martin's eldest son, Mark, and calling him jokingly 'Sir Mark'.

It could not be said that Amelia Carter-Clark was a natural mother. Certainly she had wanted her babies, and loved them now that they toddled around in pretty little dresses; but she never pretended that she had liked being pregnant, and no one pretends that they like the giving-birth itself. She had breast-fed her three girls for six weeks or so, because only the lower classes put their babies straight on the bottle, but she was glad to wean them after that and let Nanny Liddle do the night feed. She was enchanting at bath-time with the two older girls, but always dreaded Nanny Liddle's day off.

Adam and Amelia had a good marriage. The worst that could be said of them before they had married was that he was a rich bore and that she had 'been around'. Put another way, and more charitably, he was a thoroughly decent and stable fellow who needed a wife with originality and *joie de vivre*; while she was pretty and vivacious girl who had been generous with her affections before settling down. Neither had been young when they had married, and though nothing was said (in the English way), each felt grateful for what the other brought to their marriage – Adam to Amelia for her beauty, charm and amusing Bohemian friends; Amelia to Adam for the house, the money, the title and the undemanding, easy-going way in which he let her pursue her own interests.

The chief of these was art. Amelia was a most talented water-colourist, as indeed she might be – having been taught at the knee of the celebrated painter Durtling who, when he was fifty-four and she seventeen, had been her second lover. She took her art most seriously, sketching in Scotland in the summer and in France in the spring. These artistic excursions were absolutely necessary for her peace of mind, for despite a housekeeper at Parkham and Nanny Liddle, her life was very busy and quite exhausting – particularly on Nanny Liddle's day off.

There was only one flaw in her full and fulfilling life. This was the business of a son. Adam, who was so kind and tolerant in every way, became quite hard and strange over the question of an heir. He recognised that Amelia had done well to bear three children, but clearly expected her to try, and try again, for a son. It was, in the end, the only *quid pro quo* which really mattered.

When the youngest girl, Lucy, was four years old Amelia realised that the time had come for another go. She therefore went up to London (where they had a flat) to visit her gynaecologist, Mr Leedy. Now a woman's relationship with her gynaecologist is necessarily a special one, and Mr Leedy – whose consulting rooms were in Harley Street – was far more to Amelia than a medical specialist. He was calm, kind and spoke in a deep voice. He was dark (Amelia thought that perhaps

he was Arab : certainly Leedy could not be his real
name) aged somewhere between forty and fifty, and
very clean. He had a wonderful talent, so important in a
gynaecologist, of peering at her private parts, or
discussing her secretions, without a trace of embarrassment. He dated from well before her marriage, and had
helped her out of the odd scrape at a time when it was
less easy than it is today. He was, of course, very expensive.

Mr Leedy (she did not know his Christian name) was
very well aware of Amelia's desire to have a boy. The
sex of her first child had been left to luck, but before
preparing her for the conception of her second he had
explained how it was the sperm, not the ovum, which
was responsible for the gender of a foetus. If the
lighter, faster, Y sperm reached the ovum before the
larger, slower X sperm, then the baby would be a boy;
but they were vulnerable to the acidic secretions of the
vagina, and they were short-lived once their journey
was done. He therefore suggested that she douched herself with sodium bicarbonate before intercourse, and
time that intercourse to coincide with ovulation.

It had been tricky explaining these scientific facts to
Adam who like many Englishmen of his kind showed a
certain distaste and obtuseness when it came to the
workings of a woman's body. It was only when she had
likened the race of a Y sperm up the vagina to that of
Adam's great-uncle Nigel in the Charge of the Light
Brigade at Balaclava that he had understood what was
expected and had placed himself at her command.

On that occasion the analogy had been only too apt
because, like Adam's great-uncle Nigel, Adam's Y
sperm had fallen in her vaginal valley of death, and it
was one of the homunculi of the Heavy Brigade – the X
sperm – which had fertilised the ovum and created the
delightful Lucy. Thus now, as Amelia lay on the firm

plastic couch of Mr Leedy's Harley Street consulting rooms, and felt his rubber-gloved hands probe her entrails, searching for the string of her inter-uterine device, she asked him if there was anything more she could do to favour the birth of a boy.

Mr Leedy repeated his old advice about ovulation and sodium bicarbonate, and then added, in his matter-of-fact voice, certain suggestions about the position in intercourse, the timing of orgasm and the depths of penetration. All this was slightly awkward to convey to Adam when she got back to Parkham. It had never occurred to him that one could make love to one's wife other than face-to-face and toe-to-toe, and he did not quite know what she meant by orgasm. However the mere fact that Amelia had been to see Mr Leedy put him in an excellent mood. He brought out a bottle of Krug and when most of it had been drunk listened obediently to his new instructions. He was prepared to endure anything for the sake of a son, and because he was a decent fellow, he appreciated the game way in which Amelia suffered the indignity of being used as a brood mare. When he next went up to London he bought her a beautiful amethyst ring which was a handsome present for just trying. Amelia's mind boggled at the thought of what she might get if she succeeded: but it unboggled again at the thought of how ghastly it would be if she failed.

Two months later she returned to see Mr Leedy who after the appropriate tests confirmed that she was pregnant. He then explained to her that because of her age (she was now thirty-eight years old) there was a danger that the child would be born with Down's syndrome – but that thanks to the advance of science this could be diagnosed after four months or so from a sample of the amniotic fluid and, where the foetus was defective, the pregnancy terminated.

Since Amelia did not particularly want a baby anyway, she most certainly did not want what she called a Mongol. She therefore returned at the appropriate moment for an amniocentesis test. A month after that she came up to London for the result. Mr Leedy told her that the child she was bearing was quite healthy, but she sensed from the way in which his brow wrinkled into a frown that there was something else which made him uneasy.

'What is it?' she asked him. 'Is there something else wrong with the baby?'

He shook his head and then explained to her that the amniocentesis test not only revealed certain irregularities and abnormalities in the developing foetus, but also some other quite innocent facts which usually remained secret until the birth of the child.

'Such as the sex?'

'Yes.'

'And what is this one?'

'I am afraid, Lady Carter-Clark, that once again you have conceived a girl.'

Amelia burst into tears – salty tears of rage and frustration.

'Of course . . .' said Mr Leedy.

'What?'

'If the tests had shown Down's syndrome . . .'

'Then?'

'We would have terminated the pregnancy.'

'Yes,' she said: and her tears stopped.

Amelia went into a private clinic that afternoon, and was back at Parkham by the weekend. She told Adam of her misfortune – not in detail, of course – and he consoled her in that English way with nothing said. She promised that she would try again, and she did, but again, some months later, there was a second misfortune, and a second, staggering bill from the private clinic and Mr Leedy which Adam paid with resignation because he knew rich people had to pay staggering bills.

After a third misfortune Amelia seemed so downcast that Adam was on the point of calling it a day, and would have done so had not his brother come for Christmas with his wife and children including little 'Sir Mark'. His jaw then set in a grim expression which Admiral Sir George Carter-Clark had put on his face to pose for the portrait which hung in the hall at Parkham; and Amelia knew when she came back from Provence she would have to try again.

Mr Leedy was as kind as ever. He explained that the fault, if you could call it a fault, was not hers. Although science had developed methods of separating the X from the Y sperm in bull calves and buck rabbits, human beings were still dependent upon the congenital balance in the husband.

Amelia sighed, thinking of her six sisters-in-law.

'In time,' said Mr Leedy, 'I am sure a method will be found for a choice to be made, but at present, I am afraid, the best chance of having a boy is to marry a man who comes from a family of boys.

'Have you any brothers?' asked Amelia.

'Three,' replied Mr Leedy.

It is said that gynaecologists are protected from misdemeanour by the accoutrements of their profession – the impersonal consulting rooms, the plastic couch, the rubber gloves and, of course, the receptionist. They are their protection but also the source of their mystique. Certainly, over dinner at the Chanterelle that evening, Mr Leedy – or Alan, as he was called in this context – shrivelled from a lofty hero into a vulgar little man wearing crocodile shoes and a silk suit. However that was not the point: the dinner, and what followed, was merely an extension of his professional services for which Amelia stayed up in London for the rest of the week.

Moreover the treatment was a success. A boy, Henry, was born nine months later. He was a little dark – a throwback, it was thought, to the mulatto bride that Admiral Sir George Carter-Clark had brought back from the West Indies ; but everyone was delighted with him, except his aunt, uncle and cousin; and from the day the heir was brought back to Parkham Nanny Liddle called him 'Sir Henry' and Mark lost his nursery title.

Amelia was rewarded for giving birth to a son with an extraordinarily expensive necklace. For once Sir Adam Carter-Clark was happy to pay for anything – even a bill to end all bills from the gynaecologist, although funnily enough it never came.

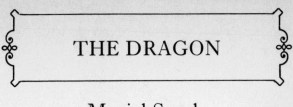

THE DRAGON

Muriel Spark

I was standing talking at a cocktail party when I was saddened to see that everybody formed a forest. I felt defeated. The Dragon had taken over.

No sooner did I feel this, than I decided it was only a temporary defeat, for that is what I am like. I didn't see then how I could possibly do it, but certainly, I decided; I was going to stop the Dragon. The party was people again. I picked up the conversation at the point where a man in the group was talking. He was good-looking, about sixty. 'My address book,' he was saying, 'is becoming like a necropolis, so many people dying every month, this friend, that friend. You have to draw a line through their names. It's very sad.' 'I always use pencil,' said a lady, a little younger, 'then when people pass on I can rub them out.'

We were in a shady part of the garden. It was six o'clock on a hot evening in the north of Italy. It was my garden, my party. The Dragon came oozing through the foliage. She was holding her drink, a Pimms No. 1, and was followed by a tall, strikingly handsome truck-driver whom she had brought along to the party on the spur of the moment. To her dismay, discernible only to myself, he was a genial, easy-mannered young man, rather amused to be taking half-an-hour off the job with his truck parked outside the gate. I knew very well that when she had picked him up at the bar across the street she had hoped he would be an embarrassment, a nuisance.

Oh, the Dragon! Dragon was what it was her job to be. She had been highly and pressingly recommended

by one of my clients, the widow of a well-known drama-
tist. It didn't occur to me, then, that the vertiginous
blurb that was written to me about the girl was in fact so
excessive as to be suspicious. Perhaps I did feel uneasy
about the eulogies that came over the telephone, and
the letters which the widow wrote to me from Gstaad
about the Dragon and her virtues as such. Perhaps I
did. But, as often when I want to believe something
enough because I am in need of help, I didn't listen to
the small inner voice which said, Something is wrong,
or which said, Be careful. I was optimistic and enthusi-
astic.

I was first and foremost a needlewoman. I have been
called a *courturier*, a dressmaker, a designer. But it was
my fascination with the needle and thread that earned
me my reputation. I could have gone into big business,
I could have merged with any of the world's famous
houses of *haute couture*. But I would have none of that.
I preferred to keep my own exclusive and small clientele. It wasn't everybody I would sew for.

When I left school at the beginning of the sixties
there were two things I could do well. One was write a
good letter in fine calligraphy, and the other was sew,
by hand, with every stitch perfect. I worked as a
seamstress, in the alterations department of a London
store. This taught me a lot, but it didn't satisfy me. At
home, I started making my own clothes. I had learned
at my evening classes how to make an individual working dummy for each client. I was very careful about
this, and I practised on my grandmother with whom I
lived. You cut a length of buckram into a body-shape
and sew your lady into it over the minimum of underwear. I did this with my grandmother, basting the
buckram on her body with only an exact inch to spare.
She thought she would never get out of it again. Then,
I slit it up the front with my scissors, sewed it up again

the exact one-inch seam. When I had perfected the sewing on the buckram with even, small, backstitching I filled the shape with fine-teased raw wool. There was my grandmother's perfect shape to set on my stand. Some dressmakers use synthetic fabrics, if they still employ this process, but I wouldn't touch them.

I made my grandmother a dress she was proud of to the day she died. It was velvet lined with silk, every inside-seam edged with narrow lace, both dress and lining. Nobody could see how beautifully it was finished inside. I have always stitched lace to my inside-seams. Even if nobody ever saw the reverse side, my clients were the sort of women who are satisfied with the knowledge that they are beautifully dressed in garments made by hand and edged inside with very narrow lace, even when a silk lining hides the whip-stitched lace-edged seams. Hem-stitch, back-stitch, cross-stitch, slip-stitch, buttonhole stitch – I can do them to perfection. No sewing machine has ever stood in my workshop. You might say it was my obsession to turn out a hand-made dress. My clients would say, 'Do you mean that you even do the long seams by hand?' 'Everything by hand,' I replied. It's been the secret of my success. You would be surprised at the demand for dresses and blouses and skirts and underwear all made by hand – I've accomplished entire *trousseaux* for clients who were prepared to give me time and pay the price.

A long time has passed since I made my grandmother's dress, and since I set up on my own. My reputation as a superb seamstress was growing all the time, so that I no longer made clothes from paper patterns but employed my own men as cutters and designers. For cutting and designing you can't beat a man; and the clients prefer them, too. The cutters and designers have come and gone over the years. I never married any of them although I came near to doing so very often.

Something within me told me not to make a permanent life with any of the cutters and designers. Fashions change so much from season to season, year to year. Cutters and designers often get stuck in a certain period, and never move on; their best work is over. Needleworkers, on the other hand, never go out of date, and I was always a needlewoman with a difference. There is a big difference between the seams that are right for velvet and those for chiffon, and I have devised ways of sewing a lace dress where you wouldn't know there was any seam at all. Lately I got my needles from Frankfurt, and my threads from London. My speciality was in the textiles that I obtained from all over the world.

So I had come to Como for silk, and was already fairly comfortably placed with my exclusive clientele. Like my textiles, they came from all parts of the world, even the wives of ambassadors from Eastern Europe. I saw a lovely house for sale on the shores of Lake Como and decided to settle there, and make a new workshop.

Now I was so well known for my hand-made dresses that I had to have some sort of protection. It takes a long time to make one hand-made evening dress or wedding-gown, so I couldn't possibly answer the telephone to all the millionairesses and their secretaries, who wanted me to work for them. Ordinary maids and *au pair* helpers were very weak, and easily bribed. They would let people in or call me to the phone just when I was stitching a circular piece or a corner – very much precision-work. My temperament wouldn't stand it. At the same time, I had learned over the years that the more you discourage your prospective clients the more they want your work, and the higher the price they are prepared to pay.

I decided to take on a Dragon, whose job it was to keep new clients at a distance, to tell them that they must write for an appointment; and she was to be very firm about this. Her other job was to look after the files of all my clients of the past, so that my business could go forward in good order, with that personal touch of remembering small items when the client finally succeeded in making an appointment. At this time I had a brilliant cutter called Daniele; he couldn't design originals, but that is a small matter; Daniele could copy and adapt. I would advise him a little – which materials to cut on the bias and which to cut, for instance, with the patterns not matching at the seams, to make an intriguing change. I usually did the fittings and pinnings myself, because I have that very exact eye. Daniele was well-paid. He was inclined to be arrogant; he felt the traditional *couture* business, where the designers employ the cutters and seamstresses, was the true thing, and that my method was the wrong way round. But I soon let him know how to mind his business, and the pay kept him quiet.

I started to interview Dragons. A sewing assistant, I explained, was out of the question for me. All the more did I need protection, and time, long stretches of time all to myself. Every stitch had to be perfect, I explained, small and perfect. Even the basting and tacking stitches, which later had to be drawn out, had to be done by me, or I could not sleep at night. Sometimes, to make an elaborate dress, I needed two clear months, working on that one dress alone. With embroidery, I needed three or four months. All this I explained to the candidates for the job. There were eight. I brought them out from England to be interviewed on the spot where the job was offered. A frightened bunch, with one exception. The others were glad to get away after the interview and profit by their trip to Italy to go and see the sights and have a good time. The eighth looked more suspicious than afraid while I explained what the job was to be. She frowned a lot. Emily Butler. Tall, skinny, with her top teeth protruding, and a lot of red hair. She understood a little Italian and spoke French, as indeed had the other girls whom I'd brought out to be interviewed, otherwise I wouldn't have brought them. But Emily: I thought she would make a good Dragon. She was to keep everybody away from me except an approved short list of clients, or people highly recommended by the clients. Even then, I was never to be called to the telephone. The client must either write or leave a number for me to call back at my leisure. Emily had brought an additional good reference from an opera singer she had worked for; she seemed to understand what was wanted. I remembered having heard somewhere that women with protruding teeth are very attractive to men, but I didn't see that this was a factor that mattered, anyway. In fact, what happened had nothing to do with Emily's teeth.

The Dragon was a marvel that spring and early summer. I worked without a break, seven days a week, sometimes twelve hours a day, frequently in a summer house in the garden except during the very hot hours of the day when I kept to my air-conditioned workroom. I must tell you about the garden and about the house.

The house was set well back from the road on a high cliff looking over the lake. It had been built at the turn of the century with many features of *art-nouveau*, such as stained-glass windows, curly banisters, and fruity decorations above the doors. From the outside, the villa seemed to have more colonnades, arches, terraces, bow-windows and turrets than its size really warranted; this means, for instance, that there were two turrets, and none would have been enough. The garden was large, really out of proportion to the house; but this suited me very well. I liked to sit and sew in the garden, especially under a mighty cedar tree that had become

my banner; you could see it from the opposite shore of
the lake, you could look down on it from the cliff-road;
wherever you were, or from wherever you approached
in those parts you couldn't miss the cedar tree. It soared
above the statues in the garden. There, on the garden
seat I would do my buttonholing in tranquillity – for I
would never sew a zip fastener into a dress – looping
the thread as I made each stitch; and if it was a blouse to
be embroidered I used to sit coolly and do my satin-
stitch or split-stitch.

In the garden were white stone statues of the period.
They represented the Four Seasons and Four Arts
(Painting, Sculpture, Music and Literature). The
Seasons were female figures and the Arts, male, but all
garbed so that it made very little difference. The Painter held a palette in one hand and a paint-brush in the
other; the Sculptor worked on a stone lion; the Mu-
sician held a flute in his left hand, with his arm
stretched out, and with the other, corrected a music
score that was cleverly set up in stone in front of him;
the Writer reclined, making notes in a book. The
Seasons were garlanded according to the time of year
they represented; their hair flowed; Winter was
adorned with holly and icicles; Spring with flowers of
the field; Summer with roses and cherries; Autumn
had a necklace of grapes, and leaned on a sheaf of corn.
The garden was very striking. Some of my clients would
exclaim over it, with delight; others would just stare
and, with a strange silence, say nothing at all. As for the
statues, they struck me as odd sometimes when I
turned suddenly and looked back at them. They looked
exactly the same as before; that is, they seemed to have
recomposed their features. What had been their expression behind my back?

The Dragon erupted in her spare time with Daniele
the cutter, and they made love after lunch in the room

off the cool back kitchen where the Dragon slept. Her red hair was growing longer and she kept it flying loose. She said it was Pre-Raphaelite, to go with the house.

In August came extraordinary rains, leaving the air between downfalls soporific and bewildered. The Dragon said to me, 'Why do you work so hard? What is it all for?' Nobody had ever before asked me a question like that. It seemed sacrilegious. I began to notice that my clients arrived late for their fittings. When you live out of town, you must expect certain delays. But, in fact they didn't come so very late to the house; rather, they were kept gossiping with the Dragon in her office, no matter that I was kept waiting in my workroom. Later, she wouldn't tell me what my clients had to say to her or she to them. I noticed that, with me, curiously enough, people started to speak in a low careful voice after they had first talked to the Dragon. When the Dragon took a boat out on the lake with Daniele, her red hair blew over her face; mostly, she came back drenched from the rain. Now, one day, I observed that she was breathing fire.

'Emily,' I said, 'I think you're not very well.'

'Can you wonder?' she said; and the smoke rose from her nostrils, flaming like her hair. 'Can you wonder? Always no, no, no on the telephone. Always, keep away, nobody come here, Madam is busy, have you an appointment? It wears you down,' she said, 'always playing the negative role.' Her nose was perfectly cool by now as if there had been no smoke, no flame flaring.

I agreed to let her invite the local people for an evening party. She brought a group from the smart hotel across the lake whom she had somehow got friendly with. She brought a number of Spaniards who were touring the lake, to make Daniele happy, and Daniele's sister from Milan also arrived. I noticed that three of my most exclusive clients were among the women who

came to that party. And there was the handsome truck-
driver. The Dragon had called in a caterer of the first
importance and ordered refreshments of the last rarity.
She was efficient.

The Dragon had taken over, and I knew it when the
forest formed around me. She came through the
people, the trees, towards me, blowing fire. Then I saw
that the statues, the Four Seasons, the Four Artists,
were wearing materials from my workroom. They were
pinned and draped as if the statues were my working
manikins, and my guests marvelled at them. One of the
statues, the Winter one, was actually wearing an evening dress that I was in the process of sewing. I looked
round for Daniele. He was entertaining the boat-officer
from the little lake port by blowing smoke through two
cigarettes stuck one in each of his nostrils. The Dragon
was drinking her Pimms, green-eyed, watching me. I
went up to the good-looking truck-driver who was
standing around not knowing what to do with himself,
and I said, 'Where are you going with your truck?' He
was going to Düsseldorf with a load, and back again
across Europe. His name was Simon K. Clegg, the 'K'
standing for Kurt. For a few moments we discussed the
adventures of heavy transport in the Common Market.
Finally, I said, 'Let's go.'

I left the party and climbed into the truck beside him
and off we went. Suddenly I remembered my raincoat
and my passport, the two indispensable vade-mecums
of travel, but Simon Kurt said, for a raincoat and a
passport leave it to him. The Dragon ran up the road
after us a little way, snorting and breathing green fire
from her mouth – perhaps it had a copper sulphate or
copper chloride basis; I have heard that you can get a
green flame from skilfully blowing green Chartreuse on
to a lighted candle. She was followed by Daniele. However, off we went, waving, leaving the Dragon and

Daniele and the party and all my household to sort out the mess and the anxiety, and the stitching and matching, forever.

Forever? Before we reached the city of Como, nearly twenty-five miles from my house, my conversation with Simon K. Clegg had turned on the meaning of forever. We parked the truck and went for a walk into town to a bar where we ordered coffee and ice-creams. Simon said he definitely felt that he didn't understand 'forever', and doubted if there was any such thing as always and always, if that's what it meant. I told him that so far as I knew to date, forever was slip-stitch, split-stitch, cross-stitch, back-stitch; and also buttonhole and running-stitches.

'You've got me guessing,' said Simon. 'It's above my head, all that. Don't you want a lift, then? Get away from the party and all?'

I explained that the Dragon was in my home, questioning the value of all the materials and the sewing, the buckram, the soft, soft silk; and the run-and-fell seams, the fine lace edging. Buttonholes. Satin-stitch. I told him about her *liaison* with Daniele the cutter.

'Her what?'

'Her love affair.'

'They should go away on holiday,' was Simon's point of view.

'There's too much work to do.'

'Well, if she's the lady in charge, it's up to her what she does in business hours. The garment industry's flourishing.'

'I am the lady in charge,' I said.

He was taken aback, as if he had been deceived.

'I thought,' he said, 'that you were some sort of employee.'

Really, he was a nice-looking truck-driver. He

pushed away his glass of ice-cream as if he had something newly on his mind.

He said, 'My sister works in a textile and garment factory in Lyons. Good pay, short hours. She's a seamer.'

'A seamstress,' I said.

'She calls it seamer.'

'I sew my seams by hand,' I said.

'By hand? How do you do that?'

'With a needle and thread.'

'What does that involve?' he said, in a way that forced
me to realise he had never seen a needle and thread.

I explained the technique of how you use the fingers
of your right hand to replace the needle and shuttle of
the sewing machine, while holding the material with
your left hand. He listened carefully. He was almost
deferential. 'It must save you a lot of electricity,' he
observed.

'But surely,' I said, 'you've seen someone sewing on a
button?'

'I don't have any clothes with buttons. Not in my
line.'

But he was thinking of something else.

'Would you mind lying low in the cabin of the truck
while I pass the customs and immigration?' he said.
'It's quite comfortable and they won't look in there.
They just look at my papers. I've delivered half my load
and I've got to take the rest across the St Gotthard to a
hotel at Brunnen in Switzerland. Then on to Düsseldorf. Health crackers from Lyons.'

But I, too, was thinking of something else, and I
didn't answer immediately.

'I thought you were an employee,' he said. 'If I'd
known you were the employer I'd have thought up
something better.'

It saddened me to hear the anxiety in his voice. I
said, 'I'm afraid I'm in charge of my business.' I was

thinking of the orders mounting up for next winter. I had a lady from Boston who was coming specially next Tuesday across the Atlantic, across the Alps, to order her dresses from my range of winter fabrics which included a length of wool so soft you would think it was muslin, coloured pale shrimp, and I had that deep blue silk-velvet, not quite midnight blue, but something like midnight with a glisten of royal blue which I would line with identical coloured silk, for an evening occasion, with the quarter-centimetre wide lace hand-sewn on all the seams. I had another client from Milan for my grey wool-chiffon with the almost indiscernible orange stripe, to be made up as a three-piece garment flowing like a wintry cloud; I had the design ready for the cutter and I had matched all the threads.

I was going on to think of other lengths and bales and clients when Simon penetrated my thoughts and ideas with his voice. 'Look, you're breathing fire. You must have some sort of electricity,' he said; and he stood up and took the bill off the table. He looked shaken. 'I can see that you could be a Dragon in your way.'

I slipped out of the bar while he was paying the bill at the counter. I waited till after dark and hired a car to take me back to my villa. Everyone had gone home. The statues in the garden stood again unclothed. Emily Butler was in the living-room talking to Daniele. I had been sorry to part with the nice-looking truck-driver. He seemed to have a certain liking for me, a sympathy with my nature and my looks which I know are very much those of the serious unadorned seamstress. Some people like that sort of personality. But when I thought of how, as Simon had observed, I was really the Dragon in the case I couldn't have gone over the border with him. Perhaps forever. Neither my temperament nor my temperature would stand it.

I stood, now, at the living-room door and looked at

Emily and Daniele. Emily gasped; Daniele sprang his feet, his eyes terrified.

'She's breathing fire,' said Emily, and escaped through the french windows. Daniele followed her quickly, knocking over a chair as he went. He looked once over his shoulder, and then he was away after Emily.

I went to the kitchen and made some hot milk. I waited there while the sound of their creeping back, and the bumps of hasty packing went on in Daniele's room upstairs and Emily's at the back of the house.

Finally, they bundled themselves into the hall and out of the house, into Daniele's car, and away, without even waiting for their wages.

My business flourishes and I manage it without a Dragon. Without a cutter too, for I've found I have a talent for cutting. I've also invented a new stitch, the dragon-stitch. It looks lovely on the uneven hems of those dresses people like, which suggest the nineteen-thirties – for the evening but not too much. The essence of the dragon-stitch is that you see all the stitches; they are large, in a bright-coloured thick thread to contrast with the colour of the dress; one line and two forks, one line and two forks, in, out and away, all along the dip-ping and rising hemline, as if for always and always.

THE MUSIC OF
THE SPHERES

A BIBLICAL TALE

Michel Tournier

Translated by Ralph Manheim

In the beginning God created heaven and earth. And darkness covered the earth and silence filled the heavens. So God made two great lights, and he made the stars and the planets. Thus there was light. But not only light, for in describing their circles and parabolas through the sky, the heavenly bodies produced sounds, a sweet, profound, perpetual concert: the music of the spheres.

Next God created man. He made him male and female, which means that he had a woman's breasts and a boy's sex, both at once. And God withdrew behind a cloud, to see what Adam would do.

What *would* Adam do? He pricked up his ears and heard a sweet melody that came down from heaven. Then he set one foot before the other, held out his arms, and slowly turned about. He turned and turned until he grew dizzy. He fell to the ground and lay there for a moment, stunned. Finally, he gave himself a shake and angrily called his father.

'Heigh-ho, God in heaven!'

God, who was waiting for just that, replied at once: 'What, my son, is the trouble?'

'The trouble,' said Adam, 'is that I can't hear that music without dancing. There are so many spheres, and their music is a regular ballet. But I'm alone. When my feet step forward, they don't know towards what; when my arms reach out, they don't know towards whom.'

'That is true,' said God. 'It is not good that man should be alone, if he dances.'

Thereupon he caused a deep sleep to fall upon Adam. And he divided his body into two halves, the male half and the female half; and from the two halves he made a man and a woman. When the two of them opened their eyes, God said to one: 'This is your partner.'

And to the other he said: 'This is your partner.'

Then he withdrew behind his cloud to see what they would do. What *did* Adam and Eve do upon finding themselves so marvellously different and complementary? They hearkened to the music of the spheres.

'Isn't that a two-step?' Eve asked.

And they danced the first two-step.

After a while Adam asked her: 'Isn't that a minuet?'

And they danced the first minuet.

'Isn't that a waltz?' Eve asked.

And they danced the first waltz.

Finally Adam gave ear and asked: 'Isn't that a quadrille?'

'Why, yes,' Eve replied. 'So it is. But for a quadrille you need to be four. Suppose we stop a while and give a thought to Cain and Abel.'

And so, to meet the requirements of the dance, mankind multiplied.

Now there were many trees in Paradise, and the fruit of each one conferred a particular branch of knowledge. One revealed mathematics, one chemistry, a third oriental languages. God said to Adam and Eve: 'From every tree of the garden you may freely eat, and absorb every branch of knowledge. But of the tree of music you shall not eat, for once you know your notes you will cease to hear the great symphony of the heavenly spheres, and there is nothing so sad as the eternal silence of infinity.'

[208]

Adam and Eve were perplexed ... And the Serpent said to them: 'Eat of the tree of music. Once you know your notes, you will make your own music, which will equal the music of the spheres.'

The temptation was too great and they did not resist it for long. And no sooner had they eaten of the tree of music than their ears were stopped. They no longer heard the music of the spheres, and a funereal silence fell upon them.

That was the end of Paradise and the beginning of the history of music. Adam and Eve and their descendants after them began to stretch skins over calabashes and hair over bows. They bored holes in reeds and twisted nuggets of copper into tuning forks. The process went on for centuries, and there was Orpheus; there were Monteverdi, Bach, Mozart and Beethoven; there were Ravel, Debussy and Boulez.

But the heavens remained for ever silent, and never again did man hear the music of the spheres.

WILDTRACK

Rose Tremain

Micky Stone, wearing camouflage, crouches in a Suffolk field, shielding his tape recorder from the first falling of snow. It's December. Micky Stone, who is approaching his fiftieth birthday, perfectly remembers touching his mother's fingers as she stood at the metal window of the cottage kitchen, watching snow fall. She was saying something. 'Isn't it quiet?' she was saying, but ten year-old Micky was deaf and couldn't hear.

Now, in the field, holding the microphone just above his head, he hears the sounds it gathers: the cawing of rooks, the crackle of beech branches as the birds circle and return. He hears everything perfectly. When he looks down at the tape machine, he hears his head turning inside his anorak hood.

Seven operations there were. Mrs Stone, widowed at thirty-five, sat in the dark of the hospital nights and waited for her son to wake up and hear her say, 'It's all right.' And after the seventh operation she said, 'It's all right now, Micky,' and he heard. And sound entered his mind and astonished him. At twelve, he asked his mother, 'Who collects the sound of the trains and the sea and the traffic and the birds for the plays on the wireless?' And Mrs Stone, who loved the wireless plays and found in them a small solace in her widowhood, answered truthfully, 'I've never thought about it, Micky, but I expect someone goes out with a machine and collects them. I expect a man does.' And Micky nodded. 'I think I'll become that man,' he told her.

It was a job you travelled for. Your life was a scavenge-hunt. You had lists: abattoir, abbey, accordion, balloon ascent, barcarole, beaver and on and on through the alphabet of things living and wild and man-made that breathed or thumped or yodelled or burned or sang. It was a beautiful life, Micky thought. He pitied the millions who sat in rooms all their working days and had never heard a redshank or a bullfrog. Some people said to him, 'I bet it's a lonely life, just listening to things, Micky?' But he didn't agree and he thought it presumptuous of people to suggest this. The things he liked listening to least were words.

Yet Micky Stone had a kind of loneliness in him, a small one, growing bigger as he aged. It was connected to the feeling that there had been a better time than now, a short but perfect time, in fact, and that nothing in his life, not even his liking of his work, would ever match it. He remembers this now, as the sky above the field becomes heavy and dark with the snow yet to fall: the time of Harriet Cavanagh, he calls it, or in other words, the heyday.

Suffolk is a rich place for sound. Already, in four days, Micky Stone has collected half an hour of different winter birds. His scavenge list includes a working windmill, a small town market, a livestock auction and five minutes of sea. He's staying at a bed-and-breakfast in a small town not far from the cottage with the metal windows where he heard his first sounds. He's pleased to be near this place. Though the houses are smarter and the landscape emptier now, the familiar names on the signposts and the big openness of the sky give him a sense of things unaltered. It's not difficult, here, to remember the shy, secretive man he was at nineteen and to recreate in the narrow lanes the awesome sight of Harriet Cavanagh's ramrod back and neat beige bottom sitting on her pony. The thing he loved most about this girl was her deportment. He was a slouch, his mother often told him, a huddler. Harriet Cavanagh was as perfectly straight as a bamboo. And flying like a pennant from her head was her long, straight hair, the colour of cane. Micky Stone would crouch by the gate at the end of his mother's garden, close his eyes and wait for the first sound of the horse. It always trotted, never walked. Harriet Cavanagh was a person in a hurry, flying into her future. Then, as the clip-clop of the hooves told Micky that the vision was in sight, he'd open his eyes and lift his head and Harriet in her haste would hail him with her riding crop, 'Hi, Micky!' and pass on. She'd be out of sight very quickly, but Micky would stand and listen till the sound of the trotting pony had completely died away. When he told his mother that he was going to marry Harriet Cavanagh, she'd sniffed and said unkindly, 'Oh yes? And Princess Margaret Rose too, I dare say?' imagining that with these words she'd closed the matter. But the matter of Harriet Cavanagh didn't close. Ever. At fifty, with the winter lying silently about him, Micky Stone knows that it never will. As he packs his microphone away, the snow is falling densely and he hears himself hope that it will smother the fields and block the lanes and wall him up in its whiteness with his fabulous memories.

The next morning, as he brushes the snow from the windscreen of his car, he notices that the driver's side window has already been cleared of it – deliberately cleared, he imagines – as if someone had been peering in. Unlocking the door, he looks around at the quiet street of red Edwardian houses with white-painted gables on which the sun is now shining. It's empty of people, but the pavement is patterned with their footprints. They've passed and gone and it seems that one of them stopped and looked into Micky Stone's car.

He loads his equipment and drives out of the town. The roads are treacherous. He's looking forward to hearing the windmill when, a few miles out of the town, it occurs to Micky that this is one of the stillest days he can remember, not so much as a breath of wind to turn the sails. He slows the car and thinks. He slows it to a stop and winds down the window and listens. The fields and hedgerows are icy, silent, glittering. On a day like this, Harriet Cavanagh once exclaimed as she passed the cottage gate, 'Gosh, it's beautiful, isn't it, Micky?' and the bit in the pony's mouth jingled as he sneezed and Micky noticed that the animal's coat was long and wondered if the winter would be hard.

Now he wonders what has become of the exact place by the hawthorn hedge where he used to stand and wait for Harriet on her morning rides. His mother is long dead, but he suspects that the cottage will be there, the windows replaced, perhaps, the boring garden re-designed. So he decides, while waiting for an east wind, to drive to the cottage and ask its owners whether they would mind if he did a wildtrack of their lane.

It's not far. He remembers the way. Through the smart little village of Pensford Green where now, he notices, the line of brick cottages are painted loud, childish colours and only the snow on their roofs unifies them as a rural terrace, then past two fields of apple trees, and there's the lane. What he can't remember now as he approaches it is whether the lane belonged to the house. Certainly, in the time when he lived there no cars ever seemed to come up it, only the farmers sometimes and in autumn the apple pickers and Harriet Cavanagh of course, who seemed, from her lofty seat in the saddle, to own the whole county.

Micky Stone feels nervous as the lane unfolds. The little car slithers. The lane's much longer than he remembers and steeper. The car, lurching up hill, nudges the banks, slews round and stops. Micky restarts the engine, then hears the wheels spin, making deep grooves in the snow. He gets out, looking for something to put under the wheels. The snow's almost knee-deep and there are no tracks in it except those his car has made. Micky wonders if the present tenants of the cottage sense that they're marooned.

Then it occurs to him that he has the perfect excuse for visiting them: 'I took a wrong turning and my car's stuck. I wondered whether you could help me?' Then, while they fetch sacks and a shovel from the old black shed, he'll stand waiting by the gate, his feet planted on the exact spot which, thirty years ago, he thought of as hallowed ground.

So he puts on his boots and starts out on foot, deciding not to take his machine. The silence of the morning is astonishing. He passes a holly tree that he remembers. Its berries this year are abundant. His mother, tall above her slouch-back of a son, used to steal branches from this tree to lay along her Christmas mantelpiece.

The tree wasn't far from the cottage. As he rounds the next bend, Micky expects to see it: the gate, the hawthorn hedge, the graceless little house with its low door. Yet it isn't where he thought it would be. He stops and looks behind him, trying to remember how far they used to walk, carrying the holly boughs. Then he stands still and listens. Often the near presence of a house can be heard: a dog barking, the squeak of a child's swing. But there's nothing at all.

Micky walks on. On his right, soon, he sees a break in the hedge. He hurries the last paces to it and finds himself looking into an empty field. The field slopes away from the hedge, just as the garden used to slope away. Micky walks forward, sensing that there's grass, not plough under his feet and he knows that the house was here. It never belonged to them, of course. When his mother left, it returned to the farmer from whom she'd rented it for twelve years. She'd heard it was standing empty. It was before the time of the scramble for property. No one had thought of it as a thing of value.

Micky stands for a while where the gate used to be. On my mark, he thinks. Yet the altered landscape behind him robs it of familiarity. It's as if, in removing the house, someone has removed his younger self from the place where he used to stand.

No point in staying, he decides, so he walks slowly back past the holly tree to his car. He gets in, releases the handbrake and lets it slip gently backwards down its own tracks. At the bottom of the lane, he starts the engine, reverses out into the road and drives away.

In the afternoon, he goes down to the shingly beach. The sun's low and the wind coming off the sea strong enough to make the sleeves of his anorak flap. He crouches near a breakwater. He sets up his machine, tests for sound levels, then holds the microphone at the ocean. He remembers his instructions: 'With the sea recording, Micky, try to get gulls and any other seabirds. And do plenty of selection, strong breakers close up, smaller splashing waves without much wind, and so on. Use your judgment.'

The scene his microphone is gathering is very beautiful. He wishes, for once, that he was gathering pictures as well as sound. The snow still lying high up on the beach and along the sea wall is almost violet-coloured in the descending afternoon. A film maker might wait months to capture this extraordinary light. Micky closes his eyes, forcing himself to concentrate on the sound only. When he opens them again, he sees a man standing still about thirty yards from him and staring at him.

Micky stays motionless, closes his eyes again, hears to his satisfaction gulls calling far off. When he opens his eyes once more, he sees that the man has come nearer, but is standing in the same attitude, intently watching Micky.

So Micky's thoughts return to the morning, to his discovery that someone had been peering into his car, then to his visit to the house which had gone, and he feels, not fear exactly, nor even suspicion, but a kind of troubled excitement and all the questions his mind has been asking for years about this place and the person he loved in it suddenly clamour in him for answers. He looks up at the stranger. He's a tall, straight-standing person. His hands are in the pockets of a long coat. In his stern look and in his straightness, he reminds Micky of Harriet Cavanagh's father, in the presence of whom Micky Stone felt acutely his own lack of height and the rounded disposition of his shoulders. But he tells himself that the fierce Major Cavanagh must now be an old man and this stranger is no more than forty-five, about the age Harriet herself would be.

Micky looks at his watch. He decides he will record three more minutes of sea and that then he will go over to the man and say what he now believes he's come here to do. 'I'm looking for Harriet Cavanagh. This may sound stupid. Are you in a position to help me?'

Then Micky turns away and tries to concentrate on the waves and the birds. He dreads speaking to the man because he was never any good at expressing himself. When Harriet Cavanagh said of the shiny white morning, 'Gosh, it's beautiful!' Micky was struck by her phrase like a whip and was speechless. Harriet had chosen a language that suited her: it was straight and direct and loud. Micky, huddled by his gate, knew that the dumbness of his first ten years had somehow lingered in his brain.

The three minutes seem long. The gulls circle and fight. Micky forces himself not to move a muscle. The sea breaks and is pulled back, rattling the shingle like coins, and breaks again. When Micky at last turns round, the man has gone.

On the edge of sleep, Micky hears the wind get up. Tomorrow, he will go to the windmill. He thinks, to-night I can hear my own loneliness like something inside me, turning.

Micky climbs up a broad ladder into the lower section of the mill. Its owner is a narrow-shouldered, rather frail-seeming man who seems excited and pleased to show Micky round.

'It's funny,' says the skinny man as he opens the trap door to the big working chamber, 'my Dad once thought of buying a windmill, but he wanted to chuck out all the machinery and turn the thing into a house. But I'd never do that. I think far too many of the old, useful things have vanished.'

Micky nods and they mount a shorter ladder and scramble through the trap into the ancient body of the mill. Light comes from a window below the ratchet wheel and from the pulley hatch, where the sacks of corn are wound up and the bags of milled flour lowered.

'We're only in use for part of the year,' says the owner, 'but we can lower the grinding wheel so that you can get the sound of it.'

Micky nods and walks to the window and looks down. Every few moments his view of the icy fields is slashed by the passing of one of the sails, but he likes the feeling of being high up for once, not crouching or hiding. And as he stares and the arms of the windmill pass and re-pass, he thinks, I must stand up tall now for

what I want and what I have always wanted and still do
not possess: the sound of Harriet Cavanagh's voice.

'All right, then?' asks the mill owner, disappointed
by Micky's silence. 'I'll lower the wheel, shall I?'

Micky turns, startled. 'Thank you,' he says. 'I'll set
up in here. Then I'll do a few minutes outside.'

'Good,' says the mill owner, then adds, 'I like the
radio plays. "The Theatre of the Mind" someone said it
was called and I think that's a good description because
the mind only needs sound to imagine entire places,
entire situations. Isn't that right?'

'Well,' says Micky, 'yes, I think it is.'

It's dark by the time Micky gets back to his lodgings.
As he goes in, he can smell the meal his landlady is preparing, but he doesn't feel hungry, he's too anxious
about what he's going to do. He's going to telephone the
big house where Harriet lived until she married and
went to live in the West Country. Though Major Cavanagh and his wife will be old, Micky senses that people
who live comfortably live long and he feels certain that
when the receiver is picked up it will be one of them
who answers. And he knows exactly what he will say,
he's prepared it. 'You won't remember me, Major, but
I'm an old friend of Harriet's and would very much like
to get in touch . . .'

There's a payphone near the draughty front door of
the guest house. Micky arranges 10p coins in a pile on
top of it and searches in the local directory for the
number. It's there as he expected. Cavanagh, Major
C.N.H., High House, Matchford.

He takes a deep breath. His landlady has a television
in her kitchen and music and laughter from a comedy
show are blaring out. Micky presses the receiver tight
to his ear and tries to shut out the noise. He dials the
number. He hears it ring six times before it's picked up
and a voice he remembers as Mrs Cavanagh's says

graciously, 'Matchford two one five.'

'Mrs Cavanagh,' Micky begins, after pressing in the first of the coins, 'you won't remember me, but – '

'This isn't Mrs Cavanagh,' says the voice. 'Will you hold on and I'll get her?'

'Harriet?' says Micky.

There's a pause. Micky reaches out and holds on tightly to the top of the payphone box.

'Yes. Who is this?'

'Micky Stone.'

Another pause. The laughter from the landlady's TV is raucous.

'Sorry. Who?'

'Micky Stone. You probably won't remember me. I used to live with my mother in Slate Cottage.'

'Oh yes. I remember you. Micky Stone. Gosh.'

'I didn't think you'd be here, Harriet. I was going to ask where you were so that I could ring you up and talk to you.'

'Were you? Heavens. What about?'

Another burst of laughter comes out of the kitchen. Micky covers his left ear with his hand. 'I hadn't planned what about. About the old days, or something. About your pony.'

'Golly, yes. I remember. You used to stand at the gate . . .'

'Wait!' says Micky. 'Can you wait a moment? Can you hang on?'

'Yes. All right. Why?'

'Hang on, please, Harriet. I'll only be a minute.'

Micky feeds another 10p coin into the pay slot, then runs as fast as he can up the stairs to his room. He grabs the tape machine and the microphone and hurtles down again. His landlady opens her kitchen door and stares as he rushes past. He picks up the telephone. The recorder is on and turning, the little mike held against

Micky's head.

'Harriet? Are you still there?'

A pause. Micky hears the door of the kitchen close.

'Yes.'

'So you remember me at the gate?'

'Yes . . .'

'I once helped whitewash your stables and the dairy . . .'

'Yes. Lucky.'

'What?'

'Lucky. My little horse. He was called Lucky. My children have got ponies now, but they don't awfully care about them. Not like I cared about Lucky.'

'You rode so well.'

'Did I? Yes. I loved that, the early morning rides. Getting up in the dark. It was quite a long way to your lane. I think it'd usually be light, wouldn't it, by the time I came up there? And I'd be boiling by that time, even in snowy weather. Terribly hot, but awfully happy. And I remember, if you weren't there sometimes, if you were working or having breakfast or something, I used to think it was rather a bad omen. I was so superstitious, I used to think the day would go badly or Lucky would throw me, or Mummy would be cross or something, and quite often it went like that – things did go wrong if I hadn't seen you. Isn't that stupid? I'd forgotten all that till I spoke to you, but that's exactly how it was. I suppose you could say you were my good luck charm. And actually, I've often thought about you and wondered how you'd got on. I was rather sad when they demolished Slate Cottage. Did you know they had? I remember thinking every bit of one's life has kind of *landmarks* and Slate Cottage was definitely a landmark for me and I don't like it that it's not there any more. But you knew it had gone, did you?'

'Not till today . . .'

'Oh, it went years ago. Like lots of things. Like Lucky and the morning rides. Horrid, I think. I hate it when things are over. My marriage is over. That's why I'm staying here. So sad and horrid it's all been. It just makes me think – jolly stupidly, because I know one can never bring time back – but it does make me see that those days when I was growing up and you were my lucky charm were important. What I mean is, they were good.'

Lying in bed, Micky waits till the house is quiet. Outside his window, the snow is falling again. When he switches on the recorder and listens to Harriet's voice, he realises for the first time that he forgot to put in a new tape and that most of his work at the windmill is now obliterated. About a minute of it remains, however. As Harriet Cavanagh fades to silence, her words are replaced by the sound of the big sails going round and round.